The legend of Father Tom O'Neil lives on in song and folklore. For those who remember, it is the tale of a young man destined for greatness. For those who remember, it is also the tale of a young man's downfall, and a price dearly paid. It is the tale of the making and unmaking of a young man and his dream.

O'Neil's Landing

Library and Archives Canada Cataloguing in Publication

Walsh, Gordon, 1941-
O'Neil's landing : the legend of Tom O'Neil / Gordon Walsh

ISBN 1-894463-45-5

I. Title.

PS8645.A468O54 2004   C813'.6   C2004-904980-1

Copyright © 2004 by Gordon Walsh

ALL RIGHTS RESERVED. No part of the work covered by the copyright hereon may be reproduced or used in any form or by any means—graphic, electronic or mechanical—without the written permission of the publisher. Any request for photocopying, recording, taping or information storage and retrieval systems of any part of this book shall be directed to the Canadian Reprography Collective, 379 Adelaide Street West, Suite M1, Toronto, Ontario M5V 1S5. This applies to classroom use as well.

COVER PHOTO: "A FURROW IN TIME"
BY LORNE ROSTOTSKI, MPA, CR. PHOTOG.
Mr. Clarence Cox (March 20, 1907-March 24, 1991) and his faithful horse Prine plough their original homestead in the Goulds, Newfoundland.

PRINTED IN CANADA

FLANKER PRESS LTD.
P.O. BOX 2522, STATION C
ST. JOHN'S, NL CANADA A1C 6K1
TOLL FREE: 1-866-739-4420 TELEPHONE: (709) 739-4477
FAX: (709) 739-4420
WWW.FLANKERPRESS.COM

Canada
We acknowledge the financial support of the Government of Canada through the Book Publishing Industry Development Program (BPIDP) for our publishing program.

THE LEGEND
O'NEIL'S LANDING
OF TOM O'NEIL

Gordon Walsh

Flanker Press Ltd.
St. John's, NL
2004

For Joy

I

The Lord foils the plans of the nations; He thwarts the purposes of the peoples. But the plans of the Lord stand firm forever, the purposes of His heart through all generations.

Psalm 33:10,11

Chapter 1

ONE DAY IN THE LATE 1800s, the morning light struck the fields and hillsides of Armagh, Ireland, and the whole county came alive with renewal and promise. Sun-dappled crops winked at the sky, while horse-drawn carriages sped with the dawn, and from every corner murmured a mingling of voices as one: mothers and fathers, sisters and brothers, merchants, farmers, lawmen, and clergy from the tiny village of O'Neil's Landing awoke to ply their trades. The two hundred and fifty souls of this small but fruitful community each greeted the other and the day's coming tasks.

Close to the town, to the north a brilliant waterfall cascaded into a river that flowed silver to the east half a mile before turning and meandering south toward lands unknown to many who lived here. Ruling benevolently over the riverbank, farm buildings, potato crops and cattle herds dotted the greenery outlying O'Neil's Landing. The farms and grazing fields crested some eighty feet above the east-flowing river and overlooked gentle slopes of verdant grasslands, whose long blades swayed in summer breezes like rippling waves on a vast lake.

Half a mile to the west of the town where our story begins, mountains grew high and surpassed the clouds that whisked by. In winter, white blankets of snow made their homes on the highest peaks. Many small streams trickled and bounced down the mountainsides year-round and fed the river in timeless fashion.

Mary Ann Jones never knew her mother or father. When she was but a year old she had made herself known to a stranger, a passer-by whose curiosity was aroused by the child's wailing. The man whose name she didn't know entered a cabin to find the baby in a poor state. On a bed to one side of the room she lay in her dead mother's arms, and on the floor nearby, her father sprawled lifeless. Witnesses to the scene said it appeared the child's father was trying to crawl toward the cabin's front door before death overtook him.

Attached to Mary Ann's soiled clothing was a note. The words, barely legible, read, "Baby Mary Ann Jones, born Aug 13th, 1 year old." The name Jones was not established in O'Neil's Landing, and none could identify the baby's dead parents.

Young Mary Ann was soon taken in by David and Elizabeth Kennedy, a couple who scraped a living at farming supplemented by temporary manual labour. David worked long hours at various jobs to provide for his wife and new daughter, returning home to work late into the night to tend their meagre crop. Although small compared to the neighbours' farms, the Kennedy homestead provided well enough for the three of them, and they were never left wanting.

Mary Ann loved the Kennedys as much as any child loved its natural parents. But the mystery surrounding her real parents' death haunted her for many years. The scant information a few residents in O'Neil's Landing had given her suggested their deaths had been mercifully quick. There had been no sign of a struggle. Contagion was ruled out as the cause of death, as the baby had shown no sign of illness. Authorities closed the case, deducing the Jones family had met their demise through food poisoning. Mary Ann eventually accepted this explanation, contenting herself with the knowledge her biological parents didn't suffer long before their deaths.

While growing up, Mary Ann often remarked to David and Elizabeth that she wanted to learn the identity of the stranger who had found her in the cabin and saved her from certain death. Her dreams were visited often by a man she didn't know. She longed to meet him and thank him for his kindness.

Mary Ann received a good education and went on to become a schoolteacher. During a school play attended by many from town, she met a man by the name of Tom O'Neil. His ancestor had founded the village and named it, descending from a long line of farmers and cattle herders. The young O'Neil was no exception, and since his father was getting on in years, the family business had been handed over to him. He and Mary Ann fell instantly in love and were wed three months after meeting at the school.

Tom's father was a fountain of wisdom. Beaming with pride on his son's wedding day, he shook Tom's hand and said, "Never look back. Don't repeat mistakes, and always look to the future." Tom would have nothing to fear, the old man added, if he trusted in God. He embraced his son and congratulated him on this most special of days.

The Roman Catholic church in O'Neil's Landing was filled to overflowing the day Tom O'Neil, twenty-one, and Mary Ann Jones, eighteen years of age, were wed.

Tom and his father had grown close after the death of his mother. The two had spent many hours in each other's company, and their bond remained unchanged after Tom and Mary Ann married. Tom and his new bride were only too happy to welcome his father into their home. His age didn't slow him down as the old man worked side by side with his son, tending to the farm and their cattle. Tom believed his father was beginning to show signs of heart trouble shortly after their wedding day, but the proud old man just wouldn't stop pushing himself.

On the day of Tom and Mary Ann's first wedding anniversary, Grandfather came into the kitchen to find his daughter-in-law preparing the table for a grand feast. Tom's father delighted in being given such a noble title. Mary Ann was not moving quite so fast these days, as she was now seven months pregnant.

Grandfather walked to the door and put on his hat. As he went out the door, Mary Ann piped up, "Grandfather, where are you going? The meal is about ready." Tom Sr. grinned and mumbled something about a little chore that needed doing, and said he would be back before supper was ready.

Soon after Grandfather went out the door, Tom came in. Mary Ann lay down the spoon she was holding and walked over to give him a kiss.

"The stew is almost ready, Tom. Why don't you go wash up?" Her husband smiled and laid a hand on Mary Ann's swollen belly before moving off to the wash basin in the porch.

As he dried his face and hands, Tom called out and asked if she had seen his father. Mary Ann told him he had gone to the barn for some reason.

"He said he had something to take care of," she called back.

Tom walked back into the kitchen. "I wish Father would lay off work, or at least slow down," he said.

Mary Ann noticed the change also. "I think you're right, Tom. For the past few weeks, he's been out of breath a lot, and the slightest thing gets him winded."

"Today is Saturday," Tom said thoughtfully. "I'll insist that he go and see a doctor for a checkup on Monday." Draping the towel on the rod over the wash basin, he surveyed the fine table setting; everything looked ready. He drew Mary Ann to him and whispered into the curve of her apron, "I'm going to the barn for your grandfather."

Within a minute, Tom returned, white in the face, with tears running down his cheeks. Between sobs he said, "Grandfather is dead." He had a pitchfork in his hand, Tom said, and he was lying face down on a pile of hay.

Mary Ann took Tom in her arms as he cried. The emotional storm passed, and he straightened up and wiped his eyes.

"Father would not want me this way," he said.

"I'm so sorry," Mary Ann said. "I had planned this meal for you and Grandfather for weeks."

She looked at the cake she had placed in the centre of the table. Written in icing were the words, "Happy Anniversary."

That Monday, Tom was taking his father not to the doctor but to the cemetery. Tom's great-grandfather William O'Neil had donated this piece of land to the Catholic church in the Landing many years before. On the wooden cross that Johnny Connors carried before the casket were etched the words, THOMAS O'NEIL AGE FORTY-NINE YEARS. Small letters beneath read, WE LOVE YOU GRANDFATHER.

When the Funeral Mass was over and the last of the people come to pay their respects had departed, Tom and Mary Ann stood in silence beside the old man's grave.

"This world is a great mystery," Tom said as if to himself, shaking his head, "one we shouldn't try to solve. But it can sure make you wonder."

He moved to a spot between his father's and mother's grave. Engraved on his mother's stone were the words, JOANN O'NEIL DIED AT THE AGE OF TWENTY-TWO YEARS. Under her name were the words, GAVE HER LIFE WHILE BRINGING A NEW LIFE INTO THE WORLD. MAY SHE REST IN PEACE.

"It was me who caused her to die."

Mary Ann touched Tom's hand. "Don't say that."

"But it's true."

"No, Tom, don't say that. Your mother wouldn't want you to think that way."

Hand in hand they walked to a double grave bearing a single stone. The marble gleamed whiter than any of the others in the cemetery. Only one word was visible on it's smooth face: JONES.

"I didn't get to know my mother, but I was lucky to know my father," Tom said. "Unfortunately, you didn't get the chance to know either of your parents."

Mary Ann didn't reply right away. She seemed deep in thought. When she opened her mouth to speak, Tom nodded. He knew what she was going to say.

"I wish I knew him. I would be able to thank him." She didn't have to explain further; Tom knew she was referring to her mysterious rescuer.

Tom looked her in the eyes, then kissed her on the cheek.

"Mary Ann, I have something to tell you. Two or three days before Grandfather died, he spoke to me about the time you were found in the cabin. No one but Mrs. Kennedy had seen the man, and she met him just the one time. He placed you in her arms and said a man and woman are dead in a cabin a little way to the south. Mrs. Kennedy didn't know of any people living down there, nor did anyone else in The Landing.

"The man told Mrs. Kennedy he had heard a baby's cry and went in for a closer look. You couldn't call the place a cabin," Tom said, looking off in the distance. "It was more like a lean-to with a small door attached. The family had been there a week at most. The stranger moved off in a hurry and disappeared.

"Mrs. Kennedy couldn't say what direction he headed. From her house she could see four hundred yards in each direction; she says she looked away a split-second, and the man was gone.

"Father said it was the work of God. He asked me to tell you to thank Him and not to look back, but look to the future with faith in God and you can't go wrong."

Mary Ann held Tom close and buried her face in his shoulder. "Thank you, God."

Arm in arm they walked from the graveyard, closed the gate behind them, and didn't look back.

Chapter 2

Had he lived until August 8, Tom Sr. would have held his grandchild. In the weeks leading up to Mary Ann's due date, Tom had grown increasingly nervous. He knew that in giving birth, women were at great risk; his own mother had given her life for his. He didn't know the exact complications causing his mother's death, and worry gnawed at him as Mary Ann's big day drew near.

When it did come, Tom was a wreck. He was ushered outside, where he paced from the house to the barn until the midwife called his name. As soon as Mrs. Hanrahan's voice reached his ears, Tom dashed around the corner of the house to find her standing on the front porch, her wrinkled face creased in a smile.

"Congratulations, Tom!" she said. "You're the father of a beautiful baby boy."

Tom's jaw dropped. He grabbed the grannywoman, laughing as he picked her up and spun her around in a dance of joy. Mrs. Hanrahan, who was seventy-five years old, batted feebly at the young man's strong arms.

"For heaven's sake, let me down. Go to your family!"

The baby was christened William John O'Neil. Having an infant in the house changed things for the better. Tom was not so lonely for his father, since his leisure time was filled with fatherly attention to the new arrival. Mary Ann quit teaching to stay at home and give her son a proper upbringing.

A year and a half later the couple was blessed with a second son, whom they named David Joseph O'Neil.

A quarter of a mile north of the O'Neil farm lived a family known more by reputation than association. The McCourts were a wealthy family of businessmen whose enterprises touched all aspects of commerce in O'Neil's Landing. Mercantile, political, and legal dealings kept the McCourt coffers full year-round, and it was whispered that not all of their dealings were legitimate. Fred McCourt, the son destined to inherit it all, was the same age as Tom O'Neil. Rumour mongers broadcasted the news that the McCourt boy would marry a woman from another well-to-do family.

One Sunday, Mary Ann was out tending to her vegetable garden when Fred's parents came by. Their lavish carriage glistened in the hot afternoon sun as they reined in their horses at the O'Neils' gate.

"Ho there!" James McCourt shouted, in a voice boasting station and power.

Mary Ann wiped her hands and walked to the gate. "It's a beautiful day, isn't it?" she said with a smile.

James McCourt sat stock-still, mild indifference pasted across his face as he took in Mary Ann's knotted hair and rumpled clothing. His own creaseless suit clung sharply to his lean frame. His wife Amy sat impassively beside him, apparently bored with this excursion among the commonfolk. The aristocrat's wife wore a long lavender dress, her petticoats rippling with each movement. Completing the ensemble was a white lace bodice, and several jewelled rings adorned her delicate fingers. Her outfit had cost as much as it would take to feed a small family for several months.

James McCourt spoke in a cool, unfriendly tone. "Fred is getting married this Saturday coming. Both you and Tom are invited if you want to attend."

With the invitation delivered, McCourt leaned toward his horses and issued a sharp command. The black steeds started away at a slow gait, but before they were out of earshot, they came to a stop.

James McCourt's voice drifted back to Mary Ann's ears. "By the way, the wedding will be held in the city."

Not bothering to wait for a reply, James cracked his whip and the horses took off at a gallop. It didn't escape Mary Ann he hadn't told her where in the city the wedding would be held.

Tom was working a lot harder these days. Six days a week he worked from early morning until late evening, and sometimes well into the night. Sundays, of course, were days of rest. After their church outings, the O'Neils returned home at noon and engaged only in essential work, such as feeding the cattle, after which they would play.

Evenings were Tom's favourite part of the day. William, who was now four years old, listened and watched as his father tried to teach him his letters and numbers, while little David tried his hardest to distract them.

Reading the Bible was a long-standing O'Neil family tradition. Grandfather did it, as well as his father before him. This Sunday afternoon, the boys returned from their room to find their father deep into his religious studies. He smiled at them when they came into the room and returned the Bible to the shelf. When everyone was seated at the table, they all made the sign of the cross and said grace before eating. When it was over, Tom helped Mary Ann with the dishes and prepared the boys for bed. He stayed with William and David until they were fast asleep, then crept out to join his wife for some quiet time.

"We had a visitor today," Mary Ann told him as he sat in his favourite chair.

"Who?"

"The neighbours from the north," she replied.

Tom sat up straight. "What brought them here?"

"They had an invitation for you and me," Mary Ann said, "to attend Fred's wedding." She continued to tell him about the McCourts' brief visit, but she stopped when Tom's hand shot up.

"There's no need for you to say any more. I know those people."

Mary Ann turned in her chair to face her husband. "You've known them a lot longer than I have," she said. "What kind of people are they?"

Tom leaned back in his chair and didn't say anything. When Mary Ann thought he wasn't going to answer her, he said, "People to stay away from."

"You don't like talking about other people, but I'd like to know about them."

Tom let out a sigh. "You're right, I don't like talking about people. If ever there was a family you should know to stay away from, it's the McCourts.

"Fred and I were friends for a while. He and I went to the same school, and many times we would walk there and back home together. He seemed nice enough at first, but I didn't like his father and mother from the very first time I saw them. I was only ten or eleven at the time, but even then I could tell they were bad news.

"When Fred was fifteen or sixteen years old, he raped a girl from The Landing. Under oath he lied that she had come to him in the field and tried to seduce him. His family, they had a lot of money. They hired Mr. Stephen Rourke, the best lawyer money could buy. The poor girl didn't stand a chance.

"Mr. Rourke put Fred on the stand first. Fred put his hand on the Holy Bible and took an oath to tell the truth. Then he told the court the same lies he had told the law when the charge was first laid. The lawyer had him well coached. And when Mr. Rourke questioned the girl, she froze up. Her mother and father didn't have money like the McCourts did, so they had no one to represent her.

"At first the McCourt lawyer tried to stop the girl from telling her story, but the judge overruled him. She did get a chance to defend herself, but it would have been just as well if she hadn't opened her mouth. She was so nervous she made a mess of her testimony. Mr. Rourke poked holes in her story, then took the hide off her when he classed her as one of the worst liars he had ever crossed paths with in all his years of practicing law. He was so abusive at one point the judge ordered him to stop. The poor girl was crying and had to be escorted from the courtroom.

"Then, to make matters even worse, Fred's parents sued the girl's family for damages. They didn't know what to do. They had no money, and they surely didn't want to go on that stand where their daughter was made to look like a fool. The only assets they had was the land they lived on. Well, that was enough for Old Man McCourt.

"That very same day, the lawyer visited the girl's parents. He told them if they didn't want to go to court they could sign the land over to Fred's father. He had papers drawn up, and advised them to sign if they wanted to avoid any more shame. The family lost everything they had. And the next day, the young girl and her family left O'Neil's Landing on foot, with only the clothes on their backs."

Mary Ann was close to tears. She couldn't believe such evil could live so close at hand.

"Now, Mary Ann, you know why I say that they are people to stay away from."

News spread that the day of Fred McCourt's wedding was fast approaching. It was to be held on this Saturday, and that morning at the breakfast table Mary Ann joked, "We'd better hurry if we're going to make it to town for the wedding."

"I feel sorry for the girl. Unless she's as bad as he is," said Tom.

In the afternoon, after doing a few essential outside chores, Tom came in and sat down in his favourite chair. Mary Ann sat and read in silence, careful not to wake William and David from their nap. She thought she heard a noise and looked over to find Tom snoring in his chair. It was unlike him to doze off in the middle of the afternoon. It worried her that he was working so hard of late, doing the work of two men. Mary Ann decided to press him to hire some help.

An hour later, Tom awoke with a start. He jumped from his chair and gave Mary Ann a shameful look. "I didn't mean to fall asleep," he said. "I'm sorry."

Mary Ann put her hands on her hips. "When you sit down for supper you're too tired to eat. I think you should hire someone, at least one man."

"But we can't afford it," Tom said, shaking his head.

She could see Tom wouldn't listen to reason, so she decided now was as good a time as any to tell him. "I'm worried you're working too hard. You have two boys depending on you, and in seven or eight months you may have a third."

"Mary Ann, you don't mean ..."

"Yes, I do mean."

Tom threw his arms around his wife and cried with delight. She laughed and cried along with him, and when they had calmed some she held him close. "Please, Tom, I don't want to lose you."

Tom pulled back from her slowly and looked in her eyes. He nodded and gave his solemn promise to hire help.

Chapter 3

THROUGH THE NEXT month, Tom worked longer and harder hours, giving no hint that he was looking for extra help or even that he intended to. Mary Ann watched with growing concern her husband come in every night looking bedraggled and sore, late more often than not. He had lost weight, and his face had grown pale and drawn.

One night after dark, long after the supper dishes had been cleared, Tom staggered into the house. He ate very little, pushing his plate away as he sat back in the chair, a thoughtful expression on his face. Mary Ann asked if there was something on his mind.

Still staring at the wall, Tom said, "Today when I was moving the cattle in closer to the mountain, a thought came to me. From the time of my great-grandfather, this land has supported one family and they made a good living from it. That's about to change. We have two sons now and a third child on the way. This land can't support three families."

Mary Ann noticed for the first time how Tom had aged since the death of his father. He was exerting himself to the point of exhaustion on a daily basis, and now his mind was burdened with this worry. A sudden chill rushed through her body. She was beginning to feel afraid for her husband's health.

"Tom, I love you very much. I know you love me and the boys. They need you, and I need you, so for Heaven's sake listen to what I have to say. Do you remember the advice Grandfather gave you to pass along to me?"

"Yes, I remember."

"Well, Tom, I have the same advice for you. Look to the future and don't look back. Learn from your mistakes and always count on God to come through."

"Mary Ann, things were different back then. My father didn't have two sons and maybe a third to think about."

"No, Tom, he didn't have three sons. He had one, with no mother to help raise him. Everyone has hardships."

Tom sighed. "All right," he said. "We'll talk about it some more when I'm not so tired."

"Do that, Tom. Our children need a father."

Tom and Mary Ann were stacking bales of hay in the barn loft when they heard a vehicle pull up to the gate. Through the barn door, Mary Ann gasped when she saw two beautiful horses drawing a finely crafted carriage on which sat a man and woman. The horses' coats had been groomed with meticulous attention to detail, and spotless white stockings adorned their legs.

Tom eyed the horses and the extravagant rig behind them. "A beautiful team," he said.

Two months had passed since the announcement came that Fred McCourt had gotten married. He was home now after honeymooning somewhere in France with his new bride.

Fred clasped his hands together over his whip. Seeing Tom admire the carriage and horses, he said, "This was a wedding present from my parents."

And too good for you, Fred, Tom thought.

He spoke up when it looked like an introduction to the lady sitting beside Fred was not forthcoming. "Congratulations to you both," he said.

"Oh," Fred mumbled. "This is Sheilagh. Sheilagh, these are the O'Neils."

Mary Ann had been trying not to stare at the beautiful woman sitting next to McCourt. She smiled warmly. "Nice to meet you, Sheilagh. This is my husband, Tom. Please call me Mary Ann."

Sheilagh held out her hand. "I'm so very pleased to meet you both."

Tom watched Fred's face darken as their wives exchanged pleasantries. The look on his face was one of purest contempt. Mary Ann invited Sheilagh to visit someday after she and her husband had settled in at the McCourt estate. Sheilagh said yes, but Fred's eyes said no. Without warning, he cracked the whip in his hand and cut off any further discussion as the horses kicked into a gallop and sped down the dry dirt road.

Tom coughed and wiped his mouth. "Fred hasn't changed a bit. If anything, he's probably worse."

Mary Ann said, "I believe Sheilagh is a different kind of person."

"If she is, and if she stays with Fred, I have great pity for her. Mary Ann, why do you think he came here today?"

"I think Fred came here to show off his new wife like she was some kind of trophy."

"From what I've heard of that family, they were all like that, even his old man James, and further back. All the women the McCourts married became unhappy and bitter."

"I think Fred had his job cut out for him. I don't think he will change this one," Mary Ann said.

Tom shook his head in wonder as he stared at the buggy moving fast in the distance. "She won't last there long."

The next day, Friday, Tom hitched up his team. The two horses weren't matched, one white and the other black with a white face, but they were strong. Tom didn't see the need for whips. He loved his horses, and they responded to his reins. He had just finished loading the wagon with goods to sell in O'Neil's Landing, when Mary Ann came out with the two boys.

William and David were always excited to go into town. Both of them wanted to hold the reins, so Tom would take them and sit them on his knees, letting them pretend they were driving the team. Mary Ann smiled as she watched the two boys playing as the horses clip-clopped their way toward town.

At O'Neil's Landing, Tom rushed into the hardware store. Mary Ann called after him to let him know where to find her and the boys. Tom was out of earshot, however, so she left them on the wagon and followed her husband into the shop.

When she stepped through the door, she saw Tom shaking his head and talking to a young man of about eighteen. "I'm sorry, Billy, but I don't need any help right now." Mary Ann could hardly believe what she was hearing. She wanted to grab the boy and shout, "Yes, Billy, we *do* need a hired hand!" Instead, she slipped out the front door without being seen.

Mary Ann was unusually quiet on the ride home. Tom watched her staring at the outlying grasslands. Finally, he said, "Do you have something on your mind?"

Fred clasped his hands together over his whip. Seeing Tom admire the carriage and horses, he said, "This was a wedding present from my parents."

And too good for you, Fred, Tom thought.

He spoke up when it looked like an introduction to the lady sitting beside Fred was not forthcoming. "Congratulations to you both," he said.

"Oh," Fred mumbled. "This is Sheilagh. Sheilagh, these are the O'Neils."

Mary Ann had been trying not to stare at the beautiful woman sitting next to McCourt. She smiled warmly. "Nice to meet you, Sheilagh. This is my husband, Tom. Please call me Mary Ann."

Sheilagh held out her hand. "I'm so very pleased to meet you both."

Tom watched Fred's face darken as their wives exchanged pleasantries. The look on his face was one of purest contempt. Mary Ann invited Sheilagh to visit someday after she and her husband had settled in at the McCourt estate. Sheilagh said yes, but Fred's eyes said no. Without warning, he cracked the whip in his hand and cut off any further discussion as the horses kicked into a gallop and sped down the dry dirt road.

Tom coughed and wiped his mouth. "Fred hasn't changed a bit. If anything, he's probably worse."

Mary Ann said, "I believe Sheilagh is a different kind of person."

"If she is, and if she stays with Fred, I have great pity for her. Mary Ann, why do you think he came here today?"

"I think Fred came here to show off his new wife like she was some kind of trophy."

"From what I've heard of that family, they were all like that, even his old man James, and further back. All the women the McCourts married became unhappy and bitter."

"I think Fred had his job cut out for him. I don't think he will change this one," Mary Ann said.

Tom shook his head in wonder as he stared at the buggy moving fast in the distance. "She won't last there long."

The next day, Friday, Tom hitched up his team. The two horses weren't matched, one white and the other black with a white face, but they were strong. Tom didn't see the need for whips. He loved his horses, and they responded to his reins. He had just finished loading the wagon with goods to sell in O'Neil's Landing, when Mary Ann came out with the two boys.

William and David were always excited to go into town. Both of them wanted to hold the reins, so Tom would take them and sit them on his knees, letting them pretend they were driving the team. Mary Ann smiled as she watched the two boys playing as the horses clip-clopped their way toward town.

At O'Neil's Landing, Tom rushed into the hardware store. Mary Ann called after him to let him know where to find her and the boys. Tom was out of earshot, however, so she left them on the wagon and followed her husband into the shop.

When she stepped through the door, she saw Tom shaking his head and talking to a young man of about eighteen. "I'm sorry, Billy, but I don't need any help right now." Mary Ann could hardly believe what she was hearing. She wanted to grab the boy and shout, "Yes, Billy, we *do* need a hired hand!" Instead, she slipped out the front door without being seen.

Mary Ann was unusually quiet on the ride home. Tom watched her staring at the outlying grasslands. Finally, he said, "Do you have something on your mind?"

Fred clasped his hands together over his whip. Seeing Tom admire the carriage and horses, he said, "This was a wedding present from my parents."

And too good for you, Fred, Tom thought.

He spoke up when it looked like an introduction to the lady sitting beside Fred was not forthcoming. "Congratulations to you both," he said.

"Oh," Fred mumbled. "This is Sheilagh. Sheilagh, these are the O'Neils."

Mary Ann had been trying not to stare at the beautiful woman sitting next to McCourt. She smiled warmly. "Nice to meet you, Sheilagh. This is my husband, Tom. Please call me Mary Ann."

Sheilagh held out her hand. "I'm so very pleased to meet you both."

Tom watched Fred's face darken as their wives exchanged pleasantries. The look on his face was one of purest contempt. Mary Ann invited Sheilagh to visit someday after she and her husband had settled in at the McCourt estate. Sheilagh said yes, but Fred's eyes said no. Without warning, he cracked the whip in his hand and cut off any further discussion as the horses kicked into a gallop and sped down the dry dirt road.

Tom coughed and wiped his mouth. "Fred hasn't changed a bit. If anything, he's probably worse."

Mary Ann said, "I believe Sheilagh is a different kind of person."

"If she is, and if she stays with Fred, I have great pity for her. Mary Ann, why do you think he came here today?"

"I think Fred came here to show off his new wife like she was some kind of trophy."

"From what I've heard of that family, they were all like that, even his old man James, and further back. All the women the McCourts married became unhappy and bitter."

"I think Fred had his job cut out for him. I don't think he will change this one," Mary Ann said.

Tom shook his head in wonder as he stared at the buggy moving fast in the distance. "She won't last there long."

The next day, Friday, Tom hitched up his team. The two horses weren't matched, one white and the other black with a white face, but they were strong. Tom didn't see the need for whips. He loved his horses, and they responded to his reins. He had just finished loading the wagon with goods to sell in O'Neil's Landing, when Mary Ann came out with the two boys.

William and David were always excited to go into town. Both of them wanted to hold the reins, so Tom would take them and sit them on his knees, letting them pretend they were driving the team. Mary Ann smiled as she watched the two boys playing as the horses clip-clopped their way toward town.

At O'Neil's Landing, Tom rushed into the hardware store. Mary Ann called after him to let him know where to find her and the boys. Tom was out of earshot, however, so she left them on the wagon and followed her husband into the shop.

When she stepped through the door, she saw Tom shaking his head and talking to a young man of about eighteen. "I'm sorry, Billy, but I don't need any help right now." Mary Ann could hardly believe what she was hearing. She wanted to grab the boy and shout, "Yes, Billy, we *do* need a hired hand!" Instead, she slipped out the front door without being seen.

Mary Ann was unusually quiet on the ride home. Tom watched her staring at the outlying grasslands. Finally, he said, "Do you have something on your mind?"

Mary Ann turned to him. "Yes," she said, "I was wondering how we are doing financially. It seems to me the farming is good and the beef prices are good."

Tom nodded. They were indeed better off than the previous year. "But I find it strange that you ask. You've never asked before."

"We're doing well enough to hire Billy," Mary Ann said. Tom opened his mouth to speak, but she cut him off. "Let me finish what I have to say, and after today I'll never mention it to you again."

She looked him in the eye as she continued. "What do you think your father meant when he said never to repeat a mistake?"

Tom shrugged. "I ... I don't really know."

Mary Ann pressed on. "That little talk he had with you was not all for me. The part about past mistakes was for you. Grandfather knew he was dying and knew he had made a mistake by not taking your advice and slowing down. He didn't want you to make the same mistake. Tom, were there times when you were growing up that you needed your mother?"

Surprised tears filled Tom's eyes. "Every day and night of my life."

"Well, Tom, think of William and David." She tapped her belly. "And the one in here."

Tom spent the rest of the ride home in humbled silence.

The summer had been good. The weather had favoured the crops at O'Neil's Landing, and Mary Ann's vegetable garden had been no exception. That year she pulled some of the plumpest, richest potatoes from her backyard. By autumn, the cellar was well stocked and the barn loft packed with enough hay to last through a long winter. Though it would be a good fall, Mary Ann dreaded this time of year, since Tom would make his annual trip to the woods to gather firewood.

Tom would cut the wood and stack it in piles before the snow arrived. When winter came, he would use two teams to haul the timber on sleds over the frozen ground. Mary Ann never felt the need for extra help as keenly as she did when Tom was away working in the woods. Thoughts of him suffering a severe cut or being struck by a falling tree kept her awake when he was away. Now well along in her pregnancy with their third child, she wished she had taken it upon herself to hire Billy.

As Mary Ann lay in bed a week after Tom's departure, she offered a prayer to God for her husband's safe return. Unable to sleep, she got out of bed and lit her oil lamp. She went downstairs and dropped several pieces of wood into the stove. Donning her heavy coat, Mary Ann grasped the lantern and went outside and crossed the yard to check on the livestock. The wind blew cold as she made her way to the barn. The dampness in the air forecast snow would fall before long.

Back inside, Mary Ann poured a cup of tea. Breakfast was hours away, but tonight she felt ravenous. She rendered out a few slices of cured pork and fried two slices of bread in the salty fat, glancing through the window now and then, praying for a break in the weather. She ate in silence, worried her husband would now have to trudge through snowbanks. Grandfather's words came to her and eased her worry as she offered another prayer for her traveller, before clearing the table.

Mary Ann was sitting by the window when a knock came on the door. She started, and her heart skipped a beat as an irrational fear suddenly gripped her. She opened the door and laughed at her own foolishness. It was Johnny Connors, their neighbour and close friend. He stepped inside onto the mat, brushing snow from his coat.

"I heard just last night that Tom had gone into the woods. I came by to see if you needed anything."

Johhny was a kind old soul approaching his sixtieth year. There was nothing he wouldn't do for family, friend or neighbour. When Tom's father died, Johnny had volunteered to help carry the casket in the funeral procession. Knowing the old man would not be discouraged from participating, Mary Ann had convinced him to carry the cross instead.

She smiled. "Some water would be nice."

Without a word, Johnny stepped outside and headed for the well. He filled the large water barrel behind the house and came back to ask if there was anything else Mary Ann needed doing. She thanked him and sent him home. He had been gone about half an hour when the snow fell heavier and the wind whistled from every corner of the house. Mary Ann was beginning to really worry that Tom might be snowed in somewhere. The mountains to the west were known for their ferocious gales and heavy snowdrifts. She only prayed he wasn't lost in the storm.

She was still at the window when Tom rode into the yard, dismounted and walked his horse to the barn. She smiled as she watched him. Tom had always said that a good horseman always takes care of his animal before himself. He would brush it down and feed it before anything else would be done. Tom had once told her, "This is the way it has been from the time of the first O'Neil." Grandfather had told him that anyone who didn't feed his livestock before he himself ate was not worthy of owning them.

When Tom came inside, the kettle was whistling on the old iron stove, and Mary Ann was stirring a pot of meat and vegetables for him. She laid down her spoon and grabbed him in a fierce embrace, saying, "I don't think I've ever been happier than I am right now."

Chapter 4

O N CHRISTMAS EVE, Tom was out of bed early. He was not sleeping well again. Mary Ann could give birth any day, and the old worry he had felt with each of her pregnancies nagged at him. The closer she got to due time the more worried he became. He wanted her to get as much rest as possible, so he crept downstairs, shoved an armload of wood into the stove, and went out to the barn to check on the animals.

In previous years, Tom and Mary Ann would visit with their friends at this time, and many of them would come to pay them a visit as well. This year they had decided to stay home as Mary Ann was suffering from back pain and tired more easily than during any of her other pregnancies. Tom didn't need to be asked twice. He wanted his wife to be as comfortable as possible.

Tom swept up the remaining bits of loose hay and went back to the house. He sat across from Mary Ann at the breakfast table and ate his ham and beans. Anyone who had tasted Mary Ann's cooking always said she was the best cook in O'Neil's Landing. He could only agree.

Tom sat back with his teacup in his hand. "That snowstorm we had turned out to be just great for me. The snow stayed on the ground just long enough for me to get my firewood and fence poles I needed home. Most years I'd be working at my wood until late February, but now it's all done. I'll be here when the baby arrives."

Mary Ann smiled across the table at him. "I love you, Tom O'Neil."

"Are you nervous about the baby?"

"No," said Mary Ann, "everything will be all right."

Tom didn't say any more. He cleaned his plate, then took his coat and hat and went outside. It was a beautiful sunny day, but cold. Half an inch of snow covered the ground. Tom began the long, arduous chore of unloading wood from his sled and stacking it near his chopping block when Johnny Connors stopped by and offered to lend a hand. They worked for two hours, and when they stopped to take a break Mary Ann appeared in the doorway.

"Tea's hot, boys, and the apple pie is hot out of the oven."

Johnny wished everyone a Merry Christmas as the two men stepped inside and stomped the snow from their boots. The old man took a small package from his pocket, handed it to Mary Ann, and sat on the floor to play with William and David. He put his hand in his pocket again, and with a look of feigned surprise on his face he pulled out two small bags of hard candy. He gave one to each of the boys and stood up, ruffling their hair as he did.

Johnny Connors loved children, and they all seemed to love him. People said he was a man amongst men and a gentlemen amongst women and a kid amongst kids. He praised Mary Ann's cooking after downing two large cuts of pie and two cups of tea. He smiled at Mary Ann and thanked her, saying that it was by far the best apple pie he had ever tasted. Wishing the O'Neil's the very best for the season, he made his way home to celebrate Christmas Eve with his own family.

With his hand still on the doorknob, Johnny turned to face Tom with a sly grin on his face. "Fred's having a big party tonight," he said. "Will you be going, Tom?"

Tom chuckled and gave the old man a knowing wink.

When the door clicked shut, Tom grinned at Mary Ann and said, "Always our first visitor."

On Sunday, Mary Ann told Tom she wasn't up to going to church. She asked Tom if he wouldn't mind taking the boys with him and leaving her home to rest. Giving her a worried glance, Tom reluctantly agreed.

Mary Ann's back was giving her trouble again this morning, and she felt as if she hadn't slept at all the previous night. Pressing her hand against her lower back, she crawled back into bed. Before long, she fell asleep and started to dream.

The boys were out, and Mary Ann was home alone with Tom. She was in the kitchen mixing bread when a knock came on the door. She opened it, and standing before her were a man and woman she had never seen before.

The visitors refused her invitation to step inside. They didn't have much time to spare, the man said.

When the woman spoke, she smiled. It had to be the most beautiful smile Mary Ann had ever seen. She said, "My dear, you will have a baby two weeks from this day, and it will be a boy. You must call him Tom."

Mary Ann shook her head. "If it's a boy, my husband wants to call him Johnny, after Johnny Connors."

"You must call him Tom," the strange woman said without blinking.

The couple turned and walked down the path, their bodies fading as they went. The door closed.

At noon, Tom and the boys pulled into the yard. They stabled the horses and put some feed out for them before returning to the house. A light lunch was ready and waiting for them on the table when they came in.

Mary Ann had a distracted look about her all day. She didn't tell Tom right away about the dream. Everything in it had been so vivid: the smells from the kitchen, the sounds of Tom eating a lunch, even the way the strangers' hair had blown in the light wind outside. Who were they? And how did the lady know the baby would be a boy? Why must he be called Tom?

After the animals' evening feeding, the family sat down to a hearty meal of fried chicken and boiled potatoes by the light of the lantern.

When Tom and Mary Ann retired for the night, they lay in bed talking excitedly about the gifts they had gotten the boys for Christmas. Tom laid his hand on his wife's belly. "The baby will be here soon."

He was quiet for several minutes, then said, "Mary Ann."

"Yes, Tom?"

"If it's another boy, would you be satisfied to call him Johnny?"

Mary Ann's heart stopped. She couldn't speak.

"Is there something wrong, dear?"

A shiver ran through Mary Ann's body.

Tom leaned up on his elbow. "What's the matter? Are you cold?"

Mary Ann's mouth went dry. She swallowed painfully. "Tom, if it's all right, I'd like to name our boy after you."

He was speechless. Hugging his wife, he said after a time, "All right, Mary Ann. If we have a boy, we will call him Tom."

Christmas and New Year's came and went. On the tenth of January, it started to snow. Tom kept a watchful eye on the storm. If it got any worse, he would have to take Mary Ann to the midwife's home, four miles away. Her time was near; Mary Ann knew the baby would come on Sunday.

At midnight the storm ended. Saturday dawned sunny and bright, the sun's rays gleaming off the new-fallen snow. Tom spent the day caring for the animals, but he didn't stray too far from the house. His wife could go into labour at any given moment.

At 4:00 A.M. Sunday, Mary Ann whispered Tom's name. She had been awake for some time, as had he.

"What is it?"

"I think you should go for the midwife."

With a startled yell, Tom threw off the covers and jumped to his feet.

"Tom, slow down," Mary Ann said. "There's lots of time. I'm not having any pains yet, but I know the baby is coming today." She shook her head. It was no use talking to him.

Tom forced himself to take a deep breath. He walked down the first couple of steps, then ran down the rest and shot out the door. The front door slammed, and Mary Ann could see him, jumping comically through the fresh snow. She, however, was as calm and relaxed as if getting ready for a Sunday outing. In a few minutes, she was asleep.

Mary Ann had no idea how long she had been asleep when a sudden sharp pain in her belly forced her into wakefulness. This pain she knew, for she had experienced it twice before, both times shortly before each of her sons had come into the world. William and David were about to have a baby brother, and his name would be Tom. And today, of that she was sure.

The sky outside was still dark. Tom had not yet returned, so she sat up and lit the lamp. Slowly she walked downstairs and into the kitchen, fired up the stove, and filled the kettle for tea. She poured herself a cupful and heaved her frame onto a chair just as the sound of Tom's horse team reached her ears. The door flew open and in he came, eyes wide.

Mary Ann raised a hand "Sit down and take it easy. I'm all right."

Tom gave her a worried look and eased into a chair across the table. "Are you sure?"

"Yes, Tom, I am." She pointed to the stove. "Now go pour yourself some tea. Where is the midwife?"

Tom froze. "My God, I don't know what I'm doing."

He flung open the door, and there was Mrs. Byrne, who had awkwardly gotten off the carriage and made her way to the door. She had moved to the area two years earlier to live near her only daughter, a schoolteacher at O'Neil's Landing. Hers was a timely arrival, as the previous midwife, Mrs. Hanrahan, had gone into retirement that very year.

She looked at Mary Ann and smiled. "That sure is a nervous man you have there."

Tom went out to the barn to check on the animals. When he left, Mary Ann told the midwife what had happened to his mother when he was born.

Mrs. Byrne said, "That figures. I thought when he came to my door this morning he acted a little strange."

"He won't change his outlook, after a traumatic event like that," Mary Ann said. "He can't."

The midwife said, "I was married once, to a good man. Much like your man, Mary Ann. He was killed in the mines when our daughter was only a year old." Mrs Byrne stared off into space. "James was a blaster in an underground copper mine."

"I'm sorry," Mary Ann said softly.

"It's all right," the midwife said. "It was a long time ago."

"Did you ever marry again, Mrs. Byrne?"

The midwife shook her head. "No, James was my only love. You know, I was only seventeen when he was killed. I was just a child myself."

Mary Ann said, "It must have been hard raising a child all alone."

"Let me tell you, it was very hard. I hope you never have to find out. But that's enough about the sad and hard things in life," Mrs. Byrne said, sipping her tea. "Let's talk about the good and the happy things in life, like having a baby.

"My dear, I know you don't know of me or my qualifications." She reached into her coat pocket and pulled out a folded piece of paper. She handed it to Mary Ann, who read it aloud.

"Frances Byrne, two years' training in midwifery, passed with honours. Signed *Dr. D. Whalen.*"

Mary Ann folded the certificate and handed it back to the midwife. "I don't know what's going on," she said. "I thought the baby would come the last of February or very early in March. Did I make a mistake with my dates?"

"Maybe you didn't make a mistake. You only had the one shot of pain; that could be a false alarm."

Mary Ann said, "No, the baby's coming today."

***

Tom came in from outside and asked if things were all right and if there was anything he could do.

Mary Ann smiled and shook her head. "No, everything is fine. Sit and have a tea and a piece of pie."

Tom looked around the kitchen. Pots of water were on to boil, and stacked nearby were clean white sheets and towels. Everything looked to be in order. He sat and ate while the ladies talked, until Mary Ann asked him to take the boys over to see Johnny.

Instead of hitching the team, Tom elected to saddle up. Johnny's farm was not too far, and the boys were small enough so that the horse would not be too burdened. When the horse was ready he went inside to dress the boys. He opened the door to find them staring up at him, fully dressed. The three of them went to the horse, and Tom hoisted the boys up first, climbing on behind them.

As they rode toward Johnny's farmstead, the oldest boy William looked up at his father and asked, "Who is that lady at the house?"

"That's Mrs. Byrne," Tom said.

David asked what she was doing there. Tom didn't answer right away. When David repeated the question, he said, "Oh, just visiting your mother." That seemed to satisfy the two boys, as they were now arguing over who would handle the reins.

They pulled up to Johnny's yard to find the old man out in his garden. He waved at the three and came over to shake Tom's hand.

"Johnny, would you mind looking after the boys for a while?" Tom asked after they had all dismounted.

The old man nodded. Tom didn't need to tell him why they had come over. "I'd be happy to, Tom."

The boys were happy to be staying with Johnny and his family. They loved his wife's cooking almost as much as they loved their own mother's, but they would never tell Mary Ann that.

Tom hugged each of his sons and bid them goodbye. He climbed on the horse and wheeled it around. He waved at them and Johnny as he nudged the horse into a gallop and headed for home.

Tom and the boys had just gone out through gate when Mary Ann announced, "The baby's coming."

Mrs. Byrne said, "I'll take you to your bed upstairs."

"No," Mary Ann said, "it's too late for that."

She and the midwife moved to the back wall, to a seat Grandfather had made years ago. It was a work of true craftsmanship, as was everything he had ever made. Mary Ann lowered herself onto the black leather chair and leaned her head back against the headrest. The midwife laid the hot water and towels nearby just as another contraction came.

In the space of forty minutes, Mary Ann gave birth to a healthy baby boy. Mrs. Byrne took him into the next room, where she washed the infant and wrapped him in the soft blanket Mary Ann had made two weeks before.

Placing the baby in his mother's arms, Mrs. Byrne said, "Congratulations, you have a new son."

The door opened, and Tom came in. He looked at the midwife, who smiled and nodded toward Mary Ann and his new son.

Gently, Tom took the baby from his wife's arms. Brimming with pride, he said, "Hello, Thomas O'Neil the Fourth. How are you, my son?"

Thomas O'Neil IV would be two weeks old come Sunday, the day of his christening. The closer it got to the big day, the need to pick godparents for Tommy weighed on Tom's and Mary Ann's minds. Tom suggested he ask Johnny Connors to be the godfather, and perhaps Johnny's sister Hazel would stand as godmother. Wednesday at the supper table he told his wife he had taken care of it. Johnny and Hazel had agreed.

At eight o'clock Sunday morning, Johnny's team trotted into the yard, Hazel on the seat beside him. Johnny was dressed in his best Sunday clothes, a navy blue suit, a white shirt and black string. His younger sister was dressed city-style. She lived in the city, and had come to visit her only brother.

Johnny went to the crib where the sleeping baby lay. He scratched his chin and looked up at Tom. "He is a special boy," he said in a serious tone to the child's father. "There's something different about him."

Tom laughed. "I don't suppose Johnny Connors being his godfather has anything to do with it, do you?"

Johnny grinned. "I don't think so."

It was a beautiful day for a ride to the church. The sun shone brightly on the crops and fields of O'Neil's Landing. Johnny's carriage kept a steady pace ahead of Tom's on the dry dusty road. William and David rode with him this morning, and their laughter echoed out over the hills and grasslands.

The little church had filled for Mass that day. Toward the end, the parents of children to be baptized were asked to bring them forward. Another family went first, and then it was Tommy's turn. Hazel took the baby from his mother's arms and with Johnny by her side she walked up the aisle and stood before the priest.

The old priest took the baby and blessed him with sacred water. He held him up and looked into his pale blue eyes. Handing him back to Hazel, he said to her and Mary Ann, "God has something great in store for this boy."

On the way home, Tom said to his wife, "I guess we have a special boy here. Johnny said so this morning, and the priest said the same after he christened him. I wonder what they see?

Chapter 5

One sunny day in March, Fred McCourt's carriage pulled up by the O'Neils'.

Fred said to Tom, "Sheilagh would like to visit with your wife and see the baby. I'll be back for her in one hour."

Sheilagh wore a heavy coat, covering what Tom could tell was a very pregnant belly. When Fred didn't give any indication that he was going to help her down from the carriage, Tom stepped forward and caught her. He levelled a cold glare at Fred. Sheilagh would have fallen if he hadn't helped her.

Mary Ann met Sheilagh at the door. She smiled and took Mrs. McCourt by the arm. After escorting her to the kitchen table, Mary Ann sat across from her and said, "I'm so happy to see you. It's been a while."

Sheilagh passed Mary Ann a little package containing a gift for baby Tom.

"Why, thank you, Sheilagh. How thoughtful."

When Sheilagh began talking, she couldn't stop. "I'm eight months pregnant with Fred's child," she began, "and I'm lonely, very lonely. Fred hardly ever talks to me, and his parents ignore me completely. Other than the servants, you're the first woman I've spoken to since Christmas. I don't know what to do."

Heavily, she struggled to her feet and went across the kitchen to look at little Tom. He was sound asleep "He is so beautiful," Sheilagh said, and began to cry.

Mary Ann went to her and held her to comfort her. "It's all right to cry, Sheilagh. A person needs to cry sometimes."

Between sobs, Sheilagh said, "He doesn't want me. He only wants the baby. I don't think I could live separated from my child. I wouldn't even want to live."

She dabbed at her eyes and said, "Mary Ann, the first time I saw you I knew we could be friends if we only had the chance. I want so badly to invite you to the house, but that isn't possible. Fred and his parents wouldn't allow it ... they just wouldn't allow me to do that. I've been so lonely and depressed. I've been begging Fred for days to let me come here and visit the baby.

"I may not have even gotten here today if it weren't for his mother. She told Fred, 'Take her over there, it may stop her whining. She'll be with her own kind.' Anyway, Mary Ann, I don't think of people the way they do. You'd have to live in that house to know what they are really like."

Sheilagh looked up at Mary Ann and said, "I'm sorry to bother you with my problems, but you are the only one I know who would listen to me."

"It's all right. I'd like to help if I can."

"This is the only way that you can help," Sheilagh said. "Fred would not allow anything more, and this may be the last chance you'll get to help me—by talking to me."

She stopped talking for a little while. When she spoke again, it was with a changed voice. Her eyes had lost all emotion. "I don't know what I'll do, but I can't stay in that house and I can't leave. I feel like an animal in a cage, waiting to be destroyed." She sighed. "Only bad things can come from a family like that." She was about to say more, but Fred pulled up just then outside the gate.

Mary Ann helped Sheilagh with her coat and saw her to the door. Sheilagh stopped, turned to face Mary Ann, and said, "I want you to know that I think of you as a good friend and a very sweet lady. And I want you to remember me as your friend. Would you mind if I give you a piece of advice?"

"Not at all," said Mary Ann.

"Stay away from that family and keep everyone that belongs to you away from them."

Mary Ann watched Sheilagh walk slowly toward the carriage and pull herself up beside Fred. Tom wasn't there to help her this time.

It was the last time Mary Ann ever saw her.

Tom was working as hard as ever. He looked tired all the time, he had lost more weight, and still he hadn't hired any help. Mary Ann didn't say anything. She couldn't think of anything she hadn't already said to convince him to slow down, so she prayed to God to look after him.

Tom was in the woods cutting lumber when Tommy's first birthday came. This year he spent twelve days and nights out there gathering the same amount of wood he normally would have gotten in seven or eight. Mary Ann noticed he was struggling to do regular chores, and he was less careful doing them, as well.

He didn't play with William and David like he once did, his patience with them slipping. Mary Ann could see he was making an effort to control himself, but she had also seen him get cross with them. This was unlike him.

Tom looked older than his twenty-nine years. But besides being overworked, she suspected there was something more serious going on. It crossed her mind to ask him to go see a doctor.

Tom was home for his youngest son's second birthday. For three days he talked about going into the woods, but every day he made excuses not to go. When Mary Ann suggested he hire someone to go with him, he stormed out and left for the woods.

This time he was gone longer than ever. Just when Mary Ann was getting worried enough to send someone for him, he arrived, at two in the afternoon. He came into the kitchen and reported that he had cut a lot more wood for fencing this time.

When Tom had gone to haul the wood, Mary Ann had sent word to Johnny that she wanted to speak to him. Johnny came as soon as he heard. The first thing he did when he arrived was pick up his godson and give him a little kiss. He loved Tommy as a son. When he laid him down, Mary Ann got right to the point. She told him everything that was on her mind: Tom's long hours, his failing health, and the poor quality of his work.

Johnny agreed. Tom did look sick. He even agreed that Tom had been getting sloppy with his work. Johnny hadn't said anything to him, though. He had been waiting for Tom to tell him what was on his mind.

Mary Ann said, "He won't, and that's why I want you to talk to Tom about going to a doctor. He will listen to you. There was only one other man he had as much respect for, and that was his father."

"All right," Johnny said. "The first chance I get, I'll talk to him."

He had in fact already talked to Tom about his health, but Tom had made the old man promise he wouldn't tell Mary Ann. Johnny felt terrible on the ride home. He liked that couple very much.

They were as close to him as his own family. He didn't like having to lie to Mary Ann.

When Tom had spoken to Johnny, he had told him that he was feeling sick. He had been feeling sick for quite some time. He shrugged and said, "I'm sure it's something that will pass."

But Johnny knew better. He had seen that colour in faces before. He didn't know what the disease was called, but it was a killer, and Johnny believed Mary Ann had seen it before, too.

Tom got home two hours later than usual, and with only a half load of wood. He put the team away, left the wood on the sleds, and barely touched his supper. He didn't wash up, and went straight to bed. Mary Ann decided to confront him in the morning.

She was out of bed long before Tom. When he came down, he looked awful. A week's growth of dark beard covered his face, and what little skin she could see had a yellowish cast to it. Before he even sat down, she said, "Tom, you are going to see a doctor. That is not a request,. That's an order."

Tom's reply was not what she expected. "Mary Ann, the only doctor we have is in the city. A doctor costs money, and besides, a doctor can't do anything for me."

Mary Ann stood up and said in an angry tone, "Tom, you don't know what he can do for you. And what good is money when you're dead? You have three sons who need you, and that should be reason enough."

Tom sat at the table and sipped his tea. He sighed, laid down his cup and said, "All right. For you and the boys, I'll go."

Tom left three days later to see the doctor. Mary Ann looked after the house and the animals while he was away. *I may as well get used to it*, she thought. Tom may work for a while longer, but she suspected it wouldn't be for long.

When Tom returned home, he looked frail and his hands had a slight tremor.

"It was a tiring trip," he said to Mary Ann and the boys. "I think I'll rest for a little while." It was only one-thirty in the afternoon. Tom slept until Mary Ann called him to supper, but he didn't eat much, and only took two mouthfuls of tea.

Tom put the boys in bed and kissed each of them good night before returning to the kitchen. Mary Ann looked worried as he sat at the table with a soft groan.

After what seemed like an eternity, he spoke. "Mary Ann, I'm dying. The doctor told me I have a large growth in my stomach that they don't have a cure for. He didn't tell me when I would die, but I know I don't have long.

Mary Ann sat in shocked silence, trying to digest all that Tom had said.

"Mary Ann," he said with tears in his eyes, "it isn't fair. What have I done to deserve this? It's not dying that's the hardest part of this. It's leaving you and the boys. Both you and the boys are so young."

Mary Ann tried to be strong. She put her arms around him and said, "Don't question God's will, Tom."

"Mary Ann, ever since I told you at the cemetery what Grandfather had told me, you've been a stronger woman. I haven't met anyone else with the same kind of faith you have."

"Tom," Mary Ann said, "it was God who set me straight, through your father, and I thank God every day for that."

Tom lowered his voice. "Mary Ann, we have to talk about my dying."

"Let's not talk about that right now."

"I don't like to have to do it either, but it's something that has to be done. I want to talk tonight. If I don't do it now, I may not have the nerve for it again. If you have anything you need to ask me, don't hesitate to ask.

"After I'm gone," Tom continued, "you'll have to try and forget me and go on with your life. You're only a young woman, and if you can find a good man who is willing to look after you and the boys, I think you should get married again."

Mary Ann let him have his say.

"My only concern is you and the boys. If you have to sell the land and move to some other place, that will be your decision to make. This land has been in my family for many years, but all things, good and bad, must come to an end. Believe me when I say I only care what happens to you and the boys.

"I love you, Mary Ann."

"I love you too, Tom."

"Is there anything you'd like to ask me?"

Mary Ann gave him a gentle smile. "No."

"Don't you have anything to say?"

"Yes I do," Mary Ann said. "Tom, I will not marry again. You're the only man for me. And the land, that will belong to the boys when they become grown men. They will decide. I love you with all my heart, and I'll miss you something terrible."

"I think we know what we want, so there is no need to talk anymore about it," Tom said. "All I have to say now is thank you, Mary Ann, for our time together. It has been wonderful."

Chapter 6

ONE DAY IN EARLY JUNE, Tom came downstairs and sat at the table. He was unable to help Mary Ann much with the chores by now. He had been a big man at one time, weighing in at two hundred and twenty-five pounds. Now his frail body weighed little more than one forty. His skin was yellow, his eyes sunken and hollow. The powder the doctor had given him for pain didn't seem to be working anymore. Tom didn't complain, but Mary Ann knew there were times when he suffered a great deal of pain.

This morning Tom had gotten out of bed earlier then he had for the past two or three weeks. Mary Ann wondered why. She gave him his breakfast, a small bowl of rolled oats with cream and sugar and a mug of tea. She knew it would remain untouched. The look of food alone would make Tom's stomach roll.

"What's it like outside?" he asked. "Is it warm?"

"Yes, it's beautiful," Mary Ann replied.

"Here's what I want to do, Mary Ann. When I was William's age, Grandfather always used to take me to our fishing hole over by the mountains. It's where we've been going with the boys every year. I'd like to take them back there today."

She left Tom to eat what breakfast he could and went outside to hitch up the team. In a short while, the entire family was driving west of O'Neil's Landing until they reached the foothills of one of the mountains. Tom scanned the surrounding area and directed them to a spot where a small stream flowed down the cliff's face to plunge deep into a small pool. The place was serene, with several pine trees encircling the natural formation.

They stopped near the small pool. Just then, a large fish breached the surface of the water and sent gentle ripples toward the shore.

Tom grinned. "He always does that. I think he's issuing a challenge."

The boys laughed and jumped around the little pool. Mary Ann handed them their fishing poles and showed them how to cast their lines while Tom eased himself to a sitting position against a large pine tree. He remarked to his wife, "God must have great things in store for me, to be taking me away from this."

Mary Ann came over to sit by him and watched the boys try their hand at fishing. "They aren't catching anything," she said after a time. "The fish aren't biting today."

Tom said, "That's all right. I didn't catch any my first time here either. It's not the fish you catch that's important. It's how you enjoy your day."

And I'm enjoying this one, he thought, *very much*.

He took out his Bible and began to read.

The day passed peacefully; the boys caught a few fish each. On the ride home, Tom said, "Mary Ann, I don't want you to make any promises that you can't keep, but I'd like you to take the boys back to the fishing hole at least once each summer, at least until William is old enough to take the two younger boys. I've been going there since I was ten years old."

Mary Ann patted his hand. "I'll try, Tom."

When they pulled into the yard, Johnny was splitting wood. Tom spoke to him for a few minutes before going inside to lie down.

When supper was on the table, Mary Ann sent William out back to invite Johnny inside. She could tell the old man had something on his mind when he sat down at the table. He glanced at Tom, who was asleep on the old leather chair Grandfather had made, the same chair on which Mary Ann had given birth to Tommy. Johnny motioned for Mary Ann to join him on the porch.

When they were alone, he said, "It's too bad, about Fred McCourt's wife."

"What are you talking about?" asked Mary Ann.

"You haven't heard?"

"No, what is it?"

Johnny hesitated.

Mary Ann was getting irritated. "Johnny!"

Johnny sighed "Sheilagh shot herself this morning."

Mary Ann covered her mouth in horror. "No, don't tell me!"

"I didn't want to tell Tom," the old man said, "but I think you should. We shouldn't keep things from him."

Mary Ann started to cry a little. Then she told Johnny about Sheilagh's visit, about how she had said living with the McCourts made her feel like a caged animal.

"She told me she couldn't live in that house and that she couldn't leave."

"My God," Johnny said, "what kind of people are they?"

"When Sheilagh visited me I thought she was just melancholy," Mary Ann said. "I thought maybe she would feel better after the baby came. Babies sometimes do bring couples closer together."

Johnny frowned. "But this family is like no other family I've ever known."

That night, Mary Ann told Tom the sad news.

"Mary Ann, the news shocks me; this kind always does," Tom said, "but this doesn't surprise me at all. Remember what she told you the day she visited. I believe she was thinking about it then. It took the poor woman all this time to get the nerve to take her own life, the only solution that came to her."

Tom was solemn, now. "Mary Ann. I'd give any amount of money and all the land I've ever seen, to live for another few years to see our sons become men. The worst pain is in my heart, but it's not my decision if I live or die ... that fate has already been made for me.

"Sheilagh had a daughter, and I'm sure she loved her just as much as we love ours. She made the choice to take her own life instead of raise her daughter, and I can only imagine the pain she suffered in her mind. But you remember this. The day will come when Fred will lose something he loves."

That night was one of the worst in Mary Ann's life. Every time she closed her eyes she would see Sheilagh holding a gun to her head. She wished the poor woman had visited her again. If only she had made a better effort to see Sheilagh, she might still be alive. But no, it was Fred and that cruel family who were responsible.

The more she thought about it, the more tormented she became. Finally, she got out of bed and went to the kitchen to make herself some tea. She sat at the table watching for daylight.

"It's going to be a long day," she mumbled to herself. Tom was too sick to do anything, and wouldn't live much longer, she was sure of that. What would she do without him? The thought of her boys growing up without a father, and the thought of the little McCourt girl tormented her troubled mind as she drifted off to sleep in the chair.

William was shaking her. "Mother, wake up!" he cried. "Something is wrong with Father."

Mary Ann jumped out of her chair and ran up the stairs, taking two at a time. She ran to her husband's side. Tom was burning up with a fever and muttering incoherently. She remembered Johnny telling her to call for him if something should happen, so she told William to get Johnny Connors to come right away.

Thirty minutes later, Johnny and William rode into the yard on horseback. The old man asked William to stay with the horse before he darted inside and up the stairs.

Tom opened his eyes and said, "It's good you're here, Johnny."

Johnny's face was stony as he said to Mary Ann, "Get the boys." When she returned with the boys, Tom beckoned them to come close.

"I want you to be good boys," he said, eyeing each of them in turn. "Do as your mother tells you. I have to go away now; God wants me to come to Him. I would like for you to go to church, and remember always what I'm about to tell you. Don't worry about making mistakes. Have confidence in God's plan for you and have faith. You'll never go wrong. My sons … Tommy, David, William … I love you.

"Now go outside and play. I'd like to talk to your mother alone."

Tom watched his sons go out the door. Then he turned to his wife, took her hand in his and in a very low voice said, "I love you, Mary Ann."

With a hint of a smile, he closed his eyes, and in a few seconds Tom O'Neil, thirty years old, was gone.

II

The Lord is close to all who call on Him, yes, to all who call on Him sincerely.

Psalm 145:18

Chapter 7

AFTER TOM DIED, folks in The Landing started calling Mary Ann the Widow O'Neil. It was a title of respect, though Mary Ann didn't like it at all. She was only twenty-seven years old. She preferred to be called by her name, and she asked everyone to abide by her wishes.

When William and David became of school age, they had begged to stay home, but young Tommy, on the other hand, couldn't wait, and pleaded with Mary Ann to let him go. After much cajoling, she spoke to the schoolteacher, who agreed to take him in when he reached the age of six. On the seventh of January, Tommy attended his first day at school, but unlike his brothers, he enjoyed learning and showed an unusual aptitude for academics.

Johnny Connors came by once a week to help out around the farm. Mary Ann was grateful. She saw that the old man was taking a particular liking to her youngest son and refused to call him by the familiar Tommy, but insisted on calling him Tom.

When school opened in September, the new teacher refused to admit Tom because he wasn't yet seven years old. He remained home throughout the fall, the envy of his brothers. Tom was excited when January finally came.

Mary Ann spent every minute of daylight working outside. Late afternoons she would stagger into the house and make supper. Evenings she would knit and sew clothes until she could no longer keep her eyes open. Many nights she fell asleep in the chair by the stove. On one occasion, passed out with exhaustion, she dreamed of Sheilagh McCourt.

Mary Ann was in her vegetable garden picking weeds. Every time she pulled one from the soil, another sprouted in its place. She looked up and saw Sheilagh standing in front of her. The woman's face was expressionless.

"Hello, Mary Ann" she said in a hollow-sounding voice. "you're still my friend, and that is why I have come to see you.

"You have never seen my daughter, and you don't know her name. Fred is teaching her all the wrong things."

Stepping forward, the apparition lowered her voice to a whisper. "In the future you will know her name and you will never forget it. I should have killed us both before she was born."

"What do you mean, Sheilagh?" Her own cry woke her up. She was in a cold sweat.

Mary Ann jumped to her feet and went to the stove. She tried to pour a cup of tea, but her hands were shaking badly and wouldn't allow it. A glance at the timepiece showed it was five o'clock. There was no point in going to bed.

An hour later, the boys woke up and Mary Ann got them ready for school. This morning she would take them to school herself and go on to the market in O'Neil's Landing. Milk, ham, and eggs were available for sale, and excess tools were gathering dust in the barn. These last items she loaded on the wagon in the hope of selling them at the general store.

At O'Neil's Landing, Mary Ann first went to the market and sold her foods. She collected a tidy sum, and smiling and humming, she made her way to the general store, where she hopped down from the wagon and began to pull out the tools. Two ladies were gossiping within earshot. Sheilagh's death by her own hand was still being talked about.

"The sheriff found a note in her pocket," one lady said.

"I heard she shot herself," her friend replied.

"Yes she did ... and I heard what was on the note."

"How do you know all this?"

"My best friend's husband knows the magistrate. The sheriff found a folded sheet of paper in her pocket, and when no one was around he opened it. The note read, 'The only way to end this living hell is to take my own life. My only regret is that I didn't do it before Josephine was born.'"

Only hours earlier, Mary Ann had dreamt this very thing. She felt dizzy, and a shiver ran up and down her spine as Sheilagh's voice came back to her. Forgetting her intentions to sell the tools, she jumped aboard the wagon and headed for home. She had to get out of there, away from town. As the wagon neared the farm, Mary Ann slowed the team to a trot and tried to settle her thoughts. Sheilagh's wish that her daughter hadn't been born would haunt her dreams for a long time.

The seasons changed and the years rolled on. The O'Neils survived the winters with the help of their steadfast friend and neighbour, Johnny Connors. When William was fourteen years old he said to his mother, "I can read and write, and that's all a farmer needs. You're working too hard; you need all the help you can get I'm leaving school to work the farm with you."

Mary Ann couldn't argue. Her hands were no longer those of a young woman, but were more like claws, scarred and galled. The reflection in the mirror showed a woman not in her early thirties, but much older.

"My reward will be to raise my boys and save the land for them," she mused one late autumn evening.

Tom looked up from his books. "What was that, Mother?"

Mary Ann patted him on the head and told him, "It was nothing, dear; I'm just talking to myself."

When Tom reached fourteen he too came to his mother to talk about leaving school like his brothers had. Mary Ann wouldn't hear of it. Immediately she called on his two brothers for their thoughts on Tom's intentions.

David turned to his younger brother. "Tom, William and I can keep up with the farm. You have to stay in school and graduate."

William agreed. "Yeah, and besides, you're not cut out to be a farmer anyway."

The older boys became men before their time, and Tom remained in school, where he applied himself with vigour, but sometimes Mary Ann thought he was pushing himself too hard. She spoke to him one evening about his studies.

Tom said, "I'm fine, Mother. I never get too tired of learning. It's like some force is driving me."

David spoke through a mouthful of ham. "I had a dream about you last night, Tom. You were all grown up, and you were a priest."

William winked at his mother. "Imagine, a man of the cloth in our family!"

Neither Tom nor his mother made any comment.

Whenever he wasn't into the books, Tom worked around the farm. On summer breaks he went out in the fields until dark and came in to read until midnight. Even though he assured his mother he was fine, she worried incessantly over his well-being. She had already seen two O'Neil men work themselves to death.

Bent over a spade in the garden one day, Mary Ann looked up to see a horse and carriage approach. Fred McCourt's team came to a stop just outside her gate. Mary Ann was surprised to see him step down from his seat and enter the yard uninvited. He gave the land a cursory glance, then looked directly at her.

"I'll give you a good price for this place," he said.

Mary Ann straightened up. "The place is not for sale," she replied.

Grinning, Fred clasped his gloved hands together. "Oh, yes it is," he said. "You just don't know it yet."

Sudden anger flared in Mary Ann's brain. She thought of poor Sheilagh, who had taken her own life because she couldn't bear to live in the McCourt mansion. She thought of the daughter Sheilagh never knew, a girl who would grow up in the twisted world of the McCourts.

She gripped the spade in her hand, and shaking with anger, stared long and hard. Finally she managed, "I think you had better leave."

Fred, who had lived a high-born life of luxury, was not used to being given orders. He didn't move and gave Mary Ann a bored look. That was enough. She darted toward him with the long-handled spade raised to strike. Fred gave a yelp of surprise and took two quick steps backward. Fury was written all over his face, but seeing that Mary Ann hadn't yet lowered her weapon, he turned on his heels and left the O'Neil property.

Once he had gone through the gate, Mary Ann's legs started to tremble uncontrollably. She lowered the spade and sat on a large rock, trying to compose herself.

My God, this is as close as I've ever come to striking someone.

When Fred McCourt reached the main road he looked over his shoulder. Mary Ann was still holding her spade. He had *never* taken orders from anyone in his entire life. And a woman! He seriously considered turning back and teaching her a lesson. Then he remembered the murderous glint in her eyes, and his stomach turned with unease.

He continued north to his home at a stately pace, and soon the Widow O'Neil and her dirty spade caused him no more distress. As his estate came into view, a plan began to take shape in his mind.

McCourt smiled. *There are other ways to get what I want*, he thought.

Mary Ann forced herself to calm down and went back to weeding her cabbage patch. The mere thought of Fred caused her temper to flare again, and several times she caught herself ripping the weeds out of the ground furiously. *Poor Sheilagh*, she thought. *How much pain did one person have to endure to choose death over living one more day? Sheilagh meant no more to Fred than these weeds mean to me.*

Mary Ann found herself getting hot in the face again, so she decided to go inside and start supper. Tonight they would have fresh meat to go with the baked beans left over from breakfast. She put the meat on the stove in a large iron frying pan, then took out some flour and began to mix biscuits. To feed three hungry young men, she would need plenty. The biscuits were in the oven when a light knock came on the door.

"Come in," she called, and Johnny Connors stepped into the kitchen. "Hello, Johnny."

The door opened again and William and David entered.

"Where's Tom?" Johnny asked.

"You'll find him in the barn," Mary Ann replied.

"That's my boy." He headed for the door.

Mary Ann called after him. "Johnny, you be back here for supper."

"I smelled those biscuits when I came in the door, Mary Ann," Johnny said with a sly grin. "I wouldn't miss them for anything."

Tom was brushing the white horse when Johnny came in. His face brightened when he saw the old man.

"Hi, Johnny!"

"Pass me that other comb and I'll give you a hand."

The two talked while they worked, brushing burrs and bits of loose hay out of the horse's fine coat.

When they had finished, Johnny said, "Tom, tomorrow is Sunday. What would you say to a little fishing after church? Just the two of us. Don't bother with lunch. I'll take care of everything. I've even got the worms dug already."

Tom grinned. His friend always knew where to find the best worms.

Chapter 8

NO ONE EVER ATE AT the O'Neils' table before thanking God for what they were about to eat. Mary Ann said the blessing, and then they all dug in. After supper, everyone helped wash and dry the dishes, even Johnny. Then they sat to have some tea, and the old man asked politely if the O'Neils would mind if he had a smoke. Mary Ann told him it was all right, so he took out his pipe and went to the stove.

Tapping the ashes from his pipe, Johnny reached into his pocket and brought out a pouch of tobacco. He filled the bowl and lit it, filling the kitchen with the tobacco's rich, sweet smell.

"Fred and his old man grabbed another piece of land," he said after a moment's silence.

Mary Ann looked at him sharply. "What did you say?"

"They got another family out of their way," Johnny said. "I'm willing to bet my last dollar that everything about that deal is not on the up-and-up."

William shook his head angrily. "How do they do it? How can they get away with the things that they do? Don't we have a law to protect us from those kind of people?"

"No, we don't," Johnny said simply. "The law of the land is for the rich and the corrupt. With money and the law on their side, they've gotten away with everything they've done."

"That is the law of the land," Tom interrupted, "but God's law is fair and just."

Everyone stared at Tom. Johnny couldn't figure out why a fourteen-year-old boy would talk this way. Looking around the table, he could tell by the others' expressions that this was nothing new. Johnny considered himself a good judge of people, but when it came to the youngest of the O'Neils, he just didn't know. Maybe when they went out fishing tomorrow he would have a chance to find out what the boy was all about.

Johnny rose from his chair. "It's about time for an old layabout like me to be on his way home."

He walked to the door, donned his hat and thanked them for a good supper. After the old man took his leave, David and William went to bed while Tom opened a book and started to read. Mary Ann bid him goodnight and went to bed as well.

Breakfast was ready and hot, the animals taken care of, and the team harnessed and hitched. Tom had dressed in his Sunday clothes and sat waiting at the breakfast table for the others to finish.

After Tom had gone outside for fresh air, William said to his mother, "How does he do it? He looks so fresh, like someone who has slept for eight or ten hours." Tom couldn't have had more than four hour's sleep. He had stayed up past midnight deep into reading, and the animals had been fed and watered.

When Mass had finished and the congregation had filed outside, Johnny came up to their carriage and said to Tom, "I'll pick you up twenty minutes after you get home.

"Some people have all the luck," David grumbled.

When they arrived at Johnny's favourite fishing hole, he cut long willows and fashioned two poles, to which he attached hooks and lines. He said to Tom, "You don't get a lot of fish at this place, but what you get are big ones."

Tom skewered a worm on his hook and cast out his line while Johnny gathered wood to start a fire for the tea.

"Oh boy," Tom cried, as he landed a large rainbow trout.

Johnny cast his line, and soon there were a total of six large trout spread on the grass. This was enough for Johnny. "We should only take from the land what we need. This stream has only so many fish to give, and if we overfish it, in two or three years there won't be any left."

Tom nodded in understanding and began to haul in his line. The old man stared at him thoughtfully.

When Johnny cleaned and gutted the fish, he passed four to Tom and kept two. One for his wife, he said, and one for himself. Tom was delighted to be able to give his mother four whole fish for her Sunday supper. They sat and drank tea and picked at the food they had brought, then Johnny packed his pipe with tobacco.

When he got his pipe going, Johnny spoke between billows of sweet, pungent smoke. "What do you want to do after you leave school?"

"I don't know," Tom said, "but I do like studying and I'm hoping to get a higher education. I'm not sure what I'd like to study, though."

Deep as a well, Johnny thought. It didn't matter; whatever Tom applied himself to, he'd excel at it.

In a short while, they packed their fish and supplies in the wagon and started for home. Tom was driving the team, while

Johnny was leaning back on the seat with his eyes closed. He raised his voice as they rode, regaling Tom with a few verses of old ballads. Tom had to agree with everyone who said Johnny couldn't carry a tune in a bucket, but it didn't matter. He just loved hearing the old man's voice.

When Johnny dropped him home, Tom asked his mother where David and William were. Mary Ann said they were gone visiting friends. "All right, I'll check on the animals."

"Fine," Mary Ann said, "if that's what you want."

Without a word, Tom left the kitchen. He pulled water from the well, enough for the animals as well as for the family's water barrel on the back porch. He went to the barn and put feed out for the livestock. Last, he split some wood and carried enough inside to fill the woodbox next to the stove.

By suppertime, David and William had returned, and spotting the tidy stack of wood one of them said, "Mother, you should have waited for us. You didn't have to bring in the wood."

Mary Ann shook her head. "There was no need. I didn't do it. Tom took care of everything."

William came into the kitchen drying his hands. "I don't know how the boy does it," he said. "I take it back. He would make a good farmer after all."

A few days later, William and David were in town for supplies when they met Fred McCourt on the street. They smelled whiskey on his breath. They turned to walk away, but Fred darted around them and blocked their path.

"Are you ready to sell out yet, boys?" he said with a leery grin

William was irritated. "Sell what out?"

"That piece of land you have."

"Our land is not for sale."

"That's what your mother said."

David made a rush for him, but William held him back. "Stop it, David," he snapped. "That's what he wants you to do."

Fred whistled and shook his head sadly. "That old widow must need a man in her bed by now."

David was wild, but William stayed his hand, steering him into a nearby store, throwing an acid look in Fred's direction as they left the street. He knew what Fred was all about. That man would have liked nothing better than a good excuse to unleash his lawyer on the O'Neils.

When they got home that evening, they told their mother about the encounter with McCourt. William blushed when he told her of Fred's personal insult on her character.

Mary Ann turned beet red. If he had the nerve to say that to her sons, there was no telling what McCourt was telling everyone else in O'Neil's Landing.

She said, "Fred McCourt was here a few days ago while you were away. He told me then that he wanted to buy us out. I had the spade in my hand, and I'm telling you he made me so mad I almost gave him the business end of it.

"You boys did the right thing. If you had laid a hand on him, that would have been all he needed to seal the deal."

David nodded. "That man has forced three farmers to sell to him already. Under no circumstances will we sell this land to him unless we all agree."

Chapter 9

IN SEPTEMBER, TOM WAS back at his studies, and every day on the road to school, he spoke to the Connorses in their front yard. At every invitation, he took his dinner with them, as grateful for the company as he was for the meals they served.

Tom was happier these days than he'd ever been, but his mother's old worries resurfaced. Her son was working far too hard for her liking. There were the chores, and inside the house every time Mary Ann saw him he had his head in his books. He had taken to reading the Bible, and she smiled when she thought of her husband's similar evening ritual. But thinking of her husband would also bring a dark cloud of worry down upon her as she remembered how he had died.

School closed for the Christmas season. When Tom passed Mary Ann his report, she was ecstatic to read he had performed with excellence in each of his subjects. With the report came a sealed envelope. Inside Mary Ann found a note addressed to her personally.

Dear Mrs. O'Neil,

It is with great pleasure I write this short letter to you. I've met some smart students in all my years of teaching, but I haven't seen anyone like your son Tom.

Besides his school subjects, he is a very, very bright student of the Bible. Tom is a person with great potential to do well in the future. He is a well-mannered, likeable young man and I wish him well in the future.

Signed,
Miss Kane

The O'Neils had a quiet but happy Christmas. The family was very proud of Tom and encouraged him even more now to stay in school.

When he returned home after school the first day after Christmas, he had news. "We have a new student this year. It's a girl, but her name is Jo, like a boy."

Mary Ann ruffled his hair playfully. "Jo," she said. "How old is this girl?"

"My age, I guess." Tom shrugged. "She transferred from boarding school in the city."

Mary Ann knew right away that this was Josephine McCourt, Sheilagh's daughter. Thinking of asking Tom to invite her over for supper some evening, she quickly changed her mind when she remembered that the girl lived at the McCourt estate. Only trouble could come of it, she was sure.

One fine spring day, Johnny Connors came on one of his many visits to the O'Neil household. He sat down to a waiting cup of tea and plate of apple pie. Johnny made no secret of his love for Mary

Ann's apple pie. He always said she was the best cook of all the cooks in the area.

When he finished the last few crumbs, Mary Ann refilled his cup and said, "Tom is out driving some cattle back in the valley." Halfway up one of the western mountains was a small valley that was perfect for grazing. The freshest grass and purest water kept them going back each year with the cattle. In the fall they would bring the small herd back to a spot near the farmhouse, where they could be cared for during the winter months.

"He won't be back until late this afternoon."

Johnny showed his disappointment. He said, "Mary Ann, I have a grandson whom I love, but I'll tell you this. I love that boy of yours just as much. He puzzles me, though. I can't figure him out."

"What do you mean?" Mary Ann asked.

"Well, it's like this. If there were three men here, and their destinies were lawyer, doctor, and banker, after an hour I'd have them figured out. By the time they were ten years old, I could tell Tom's brothers would be farmers. But Tom? I can't tell. I don't know, and that bothers me."

Mary Ann laughed.

"We'll find out in time," Johnny said, "if I live that long."

"You're a very healthy man," Mary Ann said seriously. Then with a grin, she added, "You keep coming around here, and I'll make sure you're fed." Johnny Connors was indeed getting on in years. She believed he was in his seventy-fifth year, though he didn't look a day over sixty-five.

Johnny winked. "I don't plan on retiring just yet."

By mid-June the weather had turned hot and dry. One afternoon while Tom and his mother worked in the vegetable garden, Mary

Ann scooped up a handful of soil and rubbed it between her fingers.

"It's too dry," she remarked. They had gotten very little snow that winter, and not much rain in the spring. Tom watched as his mother let the clay run between her fingers. He wished there was something he could do.

Tom stood and removed his hat, wiping the sweat from his brow, when he noticed, far off down the road, a horse team and buggy kicking up a huge dust cloud. At first he thought it was a runaway, but as it approached, he could see a lone occupant at the reins. A girl, or perhaps a small woman, was standing in the buggy, making liberal use of the whip.

She sped east, past the signpost whose thick black letters announced that this was O'Neil's Landing, and reached the O'Neil farm in minutes. Still whipping the horses into a frenzy, the girl sped on past, and finding a wide open field, circled the buggy around in a tight arc. The team trotted back toward the O'Neil farm, and stopped at the gate.

Tom recognized Jo when she first passed the farm. He couldn't believe his eyes. Never before had he seen anybody treat their animals so cruelly. He stepped forward and examined the horses. They were rearing their heads in a frantic, agitated manner, and he could see that their legs were shaking badly.

"Jo," he said in a firm voice, "if you don't let this team rest, *and* walk them home, you'll surely kill them."

He fetched a bucket of water from the well and gave a little to the winded horses. "Jo," he repeated, "you have to let these horses rest."

The young girl laughed and tossed her hair. "It's all right. There are plenty of horses at our place."

Tom gave her an incredulous look.

"Tom," said Jo sweetly, "there's going to be a party at my house on Saturday night. You're welcome to join us. It's my birthday." With that, Miss McCourt wheeled her team around and sent them into a gallop toward home.

Mary Ann walked up to Tom, who was shaking his head in disbelief. "If they make it home they'll probably have to be put down," he said.

His mother had been watching this exchange from a distance. She hadn't taken her eyes off the girl for a second. She couldn't have even if she wanted to. Jo had been drawing her gaze like a magnet.

She was a beautiful young woman who had inherited her mother's fine features, but her imperious demeanour was all Fred. She wanted to warn Tom to stay as far away from her as possible, but how could a boy understand such things? Instead, she went back to her cabbage patch and uttered a silent prayer that Tom, and her other sons for that matter, would use good judgment when dealing with this one.

When Tom started school again in the fall, neither he nor his mother knew it would be his last year. He pored over his books day and night, and as Mary Ann observed him among his piles of books, the difference between him and his brothers was mystifying.

Christmas came with no snow. The vegetation the previous year had suffered, resulting in sales so low Mary Ann had begun to seriously wonder if they would have to sell the farm. Luck was with them though, as was Johnny Connors, and somehow they survived.

Two days before Tom's sixteenth birthday, Mary Ann decided to contact his schoolmates and invite them to a surprise party. All, that is, but Josephine McCourt. Never in her life had Mary Ann turned anyone away at her door, but this girl was a troublemaker.

On the day of the party, however, Jo McCourt couldn't be contained, strutting into the house as if she owned the place. She flashed a smile at Tom and his mother, dumped her gift on the table with the others, and helped herself to a plate of sandwiches. Mary Ann scowled, but she was determined not to make a scene.

Jo took care of that for her. The guests were enjoying their last get-together before school reopened, when young Miss McCourt started upsetting some of the boys and girls. Mary Ann watched as the girl went around the room, whispering, pointing to this one or that one and throwing glances, hoping to intimidate or provoke a hostile confontation. A couple of classmates actually gave Tom cold stares before leaving early. It chilled Mary Ann to see someone so young cause so much distress.

The next morning, Mary Ann was still upset. While sweeping up she said, "I'm sorry your party was ruined, Tom."

"It's all right, Mother, it wasn't your fault. You couldn't have known she was going to upset my friends. Besides, I think most of them saw right through her."

Mary Ann stopped sweeping. "You'd think I invited Jo to the party," she said, "the way she pranced in."

Tom raised his eyebrows. "You didn't?"

"No," said Mary Ann surprised. "Did you?"

"No." Tom shook his head. "Now doesn't that beat all!"

Mary Ann decided then and there to have a little talk. "Tom, sit down and I'll pour you a cup of tea. There's something I want to tell you."

When they were both seated, Mary Ann took her son's hand and looked into his eyes.

"Tom, I'll come right to the point. I want you to stay away from Jo. I think she is trouble, and very bad trouble. I wanted to tell you that for a long time now, but I didn't feel at the time I had a good enough reason."

Tom nodded slowly. "None of the students in the school can get along with her," he said. "She's always making trouble for someone. All right, Mother, I'll do as you wish."

Johnny came over later that day. He had been invited to the party, of course, but had refused to come. "Ah, an old fella like me would just spoil the party," he had said. Wishing Tom a happy birthday, he handed over a small, tightly wrapped package. The old man grinned when he saw Tom's eyes widen at the sight of the gold watch and chain he pulled from the paper.

Tom laughed and jumped into the air, and threw his arms around Johnny and hugged him fiercely. Finally, unable to stand it anymore, Johnny wheezed, "Turn it over."

On the back was engraved, TO THE BEST FRIEND I EVER HAD. JOHNNY.

It was late February before enough snow came for William and David to transport the firewood home. It was beginning to look as if this year would be like the last, until the fifth of March, when the sky clouded over and the wind started to blow from the northeast. It was what Johnny Connors referred to as the snow-wind in winter, and the rain-wind in the summer.

It snowed on the fifth and didn't stop for two days. The residents of O'Neil's Landing welcomed the tumultuous weather. The storm and ensuing snowfall heralded rainy days in the spring and summer. The crops would yield vegetables aplenty, and many a farmer along the river breathed a sigh of relief.

The day before school closed, Tom had told his mother that his teacher wanted to talk to her. Mary Ann asked him if he knew why, but Tom only shook his head. The next day Mary Ann drove the team out to the schoolhouse to find out what was on Miss Kane's mind. She didn't know the teacher very well, but what she did know of her she liked.

Miss Kane greeted Mary Ann when she arrived and asked her to take a seat. "Mrs. O'Neil," she began, "I wanted to speak to you regarding your son."

"Why? Is there something wrong?"

"Oh, no," said the schoolteacher. "I just wanted to tell you that there is no reason for Tom to come back to school in the fall."

"Why not?" Mary Ann asked alarmed.

"Well," said Miss Kane, "we can't do any more for him. This school can't teach him anything else. What I'm trying to tell you is that Tom could teach me now, and I'm proud to be able to say that to you. Besides being the smartest student I have ever taught, he is the best in character. I don't know what Tom has in mind, but I'm sure he'll excel at whatever it might be."

Mary Ann was ecstatic. Her heart almost burst with pride for her youngest son. He had really outdone himself, but Mary Ann also felt a momentary twinge of sadness. They were not wealthy, and they couldn't afford to send him elsewhere to further educate him. She said as much to the schoolteacher.

Miss Kane tapped her chin thoughtfully. "This is not absolute yet," she said after some time, "but the school may be giving Bible lessons next year."

"What does that have to do with Tom? He's not a teacher."

"No," said Miss Kane, "he isn't. But he most certainly could be. I have never seen anyone who knows as much about the subject.

You should encourage him to apply for the position. I can't guarantee anything, but I'll do whatever I can. I'll talk to the school board and recommend that he get the job."

Mary Ann was touched. She shook the schoolteacher's hand and thanked her. "I'll talk to Tom when he comes home," she said.

Miss Kane returned her smile and said, "You can do that on your way home. There is no reason for Tom to be here anymore. I had a talk with Tom before you came; now all I have to do is hand him what will be the best report I've ever handed out.

"Mrs. O'Neil, I know you're proud of him. If it were the other way around, and I were passing Tom a poor report, you'd still be proud of him. That's the kind of woman you are. It's easy to tell where Tom gets his kind ways. I wish both you and Tom the very best in the future."

On the way home, Mary Ann told Tom of the meeting with Miss Kane.

"She wants to know if you'd be interested in teaching. There may be Bible classes offered this coming fall and she thinks you're the right person for the job. You should apply."

"I'd love to, Mother."

With the young men doing the majority of the chores around the farm, Mary Ann didn't have to work as hard as she used to, but she still kept herself busy. Besides all the work around the house, she pitched in with splitting the firewood and keeping the animals clean and fed. Tom also helped her whenever there was any heavy lifting to be done.

One morning, the family was sitting around the table when Tom announced he would like to apply for the position at the school. He asked the others if they were all right with it. Mary Ann looked at the others and answered for them.

"Of course, Tom. You should."

William, who was now twenty years old, clapped his youngest brother on the back and told him the farm would still be in good hands.

"All right then, that's settled," Tom said. He added, "But I may not get the position, you know."

Tom left home the last week in August for an overnight stay up in the valley where they kept their cattle. This was a monthly routine usually handled by David, but Tom volunteered to go this time. Years before Tom was born, his grandfather kept his cattle in the same valley. He had forty at a time, which he herded to the valley in late May or early June. Grandfather had stayed overnight once and the next day rode around the area looking for signs of predators. Satisfied his cattle were not in danger, he had left for home. Before he could return to the valley, he came down with pneumonia and was bedridden for over a month. When he did return, he found the herd wiped out. Rotting carcasses littered the grassy field. That was the closest Grandfather had ever come to losing his land. They never did find out the cause of the deaths, though tracks from mountain cats were found nearby.

When Tom returned home, he found a letter waiting for him. He opened it and handed it to his mother without reading it. A smile spread across Mary Ann's face at once. The letter had come from the school and was signed by Miss Kane. She had written the letter to congratulate Tom on his new position.

Tom could hardly wait for school to start. This meant more money for the family. When he received his first payment, he would buy something, not for himself, but for his mother. At the general store in O'Neil's Landing he had seen her admire a dress, but they couldn't afford it.

He grinned. The faded old grey dress his mother wore to church on Sundays just wouldn't do anymore.

Tom started teaching in September. At the end of every month he would be paid a modest sum. By Christmas he had saved enough to buy presents for everybody. It thrilled him to be able to use money he had earned from his own hard work. He wrapped his mother's gift in fancy paper, then signed it FROM WILLIAM, DAVID, AND TOM. On the night of Christmas Eve, he and his brothers stood around the kitchen and called for their mother to come down.

Tom placed the package in the centre of the table when Mary Ann was seated.

David said, "We elected Tom to speak for all of us."

Tom took a mouthful of tea, swallowed, and said, "Mother, we can only imagine the hardships you must have gone through after Father died. You were left with three small sons and a farm to run. We can remember some of the days and nights you went without much yourself, to look after us."

Tom exchanged glances with his brothers, then turning back to Mary Ann he said, "Mother, we love you and we have a little surprise for you."

William said, "Open it, Mother. It may need a little work done on it before church tomorrow."

William, David and Tom were waiting by the stairs the next morning when their mother came down. When she reached them, she did a slow turn in her new dress.

"Mother," Tom said, "you're the most beautiful woman in all of Ireland."

Chapter 10

OVER THE NEXT TWO years, the students at the O'Neil's Landing schoolhouse came to respect their new teacher.

But all was not well.

Fred McCourt, whose political machinations reached far and wide, made it known to his associates that he was displeased with all the attention the O'Neil boy had been receiving. In Tom's third year, when the time came for election of school board members, Fred's name appeared first on the list of candidates. It was rumoured that he had hired several of his own men to run, and that a friend on the current board threatened others to abstain.

A week before school opened, Tom received a letter from the board stating that his services were no longer required. The letter was signed, "Fred McCourt, President."

Two days later, while Mary Ann was outside tending her garden, she spied a horse and buggy approaching the farm. As it drew nearer, she saw that its lone occupant was a woman.

When the rig came to a stop by her gate, Mary Ann approached and said, "Please, Miss Kane, get down and come in the house."

Mary Ann noticed wooden boxes and a large trunk behind the buggy's seat. She asked, "Are you going somewhere?"

"Yes," Miss Kane said as she hopped down. "I'm leaving O'Neil's Landing."

"I see. Please, Miss Kane, come inside."

Mary Ann put the kettle on the stove, then both ladies sat at the table. Mary Ann asked, "Why are you leaving?"

"I've tried to reason with the board," Miss Kane said angrily. She fell silent for a moment. "I shouldn't say the board," she continued. "I should say Fred. It seems *he* is the board."

"You're not leaving for good, are you?" Mary Ann interrupted.

Miss Kane raised her eyebrows. "You haven't heard? I've been fired, too. They can easily replace me, but what they did to Tom was unforgivable. You can't replace someone like him. Fred had me fired because his daughter was causing trouble and I wouldn't stand for it.

"Before he was president, he wanted me to lie for her, but I refused. At the time he couldn't do very much about it. He tried, though. He wanted the board to get rid of me, but they wouldn't hear of it. But now it's a one-man show and he's the boss, Mrs. O'Neil."

"Please call me Mary Ann." She set about pouring tea.

"All right, Mary Ann. If this were my hometown, I'd stand up to him. I mightn't win, but I'd have the satisfaction of having tried.

"I've met many people in my twenty-five years of teaching, but I've never met anyone like Fred and Jo. I believe that if someone doesn't stand up to them, they are going to cause some serious trouble.

"I didn't come here with the intention of retiring, but to get away from the city during my last few years of my career. It's time for me to go back. I am sorry. I didn't stop to burden you with my troubles. I just wanted to say goodbye to Tom and to wish him luck in the future. Since he isn't here, I'd like for you to pass it on to him. Tell him I'll drop a line when I get settled. Thank you for the tea."

Miss Kane went out and climbed aboard the buggy. "Goodbye, Mary Ann. It was nice to get to know you and your family."

"It was nice knowing you, too," Mary Ann said in a far-off voice.

The schoolteacher gave a soft command to her horse, and away she went. She waved to Mary Ann, and then was gone from O'Neil's Landing.

When Tom came home that evening his mother told him of Miss Kane's visit to wish him well.

"She was one fine teacher. I'm sure she'll have no trouble finding another school," Tom said.

"She says someone ought to stand up to Fred and his crooked dealings."

Tom nodded. "I think she's right. That time will come." His voice took on a strange quality. "I'm not nineteen years old and already I've been fired from my first job."

Tom slaved at the farm chores all that year. In the fall, he volunteered to go alone to the woods and cut their firewood.

William asked him, "Why by yourself?"

"I want to experience some of the things alone that my father did," Tom replied, and no more was said about it.

When the time came, Tom packed his Bible and a week's supply of food, and stowed a saw and an axe in a light backpack. He left very early on Monday morning with two pack horses. For the entire week he worked each waking minute of every day, from first light until the stars lit up the night sky. Tom was a big, strong man who never tired. After a long, gruelling day of chopping wood, he would make supper and then spend an hour reading.

When he had finished cutting and piling the wood Saturday evening, the sky clouded over and a light rain began to fall. He returned to camp and cooked his supper, then started gathering his tools and the remainder of his provisions. It was going to be a bad night, but he wanted to keep his promise and be home in time for church tomorrow.

Pulling up to the barn door at midnight, Tom lowered himself to the ground, trying to make as little noise as possible. He unstrapped one pack when a voice suddenly cut through the night air.

"Tom O'Neil is the only man I know who would ride all night in a storm to go to church."

Tom said, "I'm sorry I woke you, David."

"You didn't wake me," he said. "I was waiting for you. Here, let me help you with that other pack."

"And how did you know I'd be home tonight?"

"Mother said you'd be home for church on Sunday," David said, "and I know my brother. He always keeps his word."

After a good night's sleep, Tom rose at first light and filled the woodstove. He heated the kettle, downed a quick cup of tea, and headed for the barn. The smell of ham and potatoes frying brought him back inside an hour later. He sat at the table just as his brothers entered the kitchen.

"Welcome home, brother," William said with a yawn. "Don't you ever sleep? You're always out of bed before me, and half a day's work is done before anyone else is even awake. I'd sure hate to lose you."

"Leave the dishes, Mother," David said. "You go and put on that new dress."

Tom got up and carried his plate to the counter. William waved a hand at him. "Tom, you sit. We'll clean up while you tell us about your trip to the woods."

Tom nodded and sat back down. "I enjoyed being out in the woods alone. The smell of the forest and the silence when the wind isn't blowing is very peaceful. Lying down under the stars after supper gives a man a chance to think."

When he finished telling the others about his week, Tom left the kitchen and went out to the barn. He harnessed the team to the carriage and saddled a horse for himself to ride to Johnny Connors's place after church. Back inside the house, his gaze fell on his mother wearing the dress he had given her for Christmas. "Mother, you look fifteen years younger."

The family was surprised to see a new priest deliver the sermon that day. He preached on the virtue of forgiveness and after Mass stood at the front door to greet and shake hands with the congregation as they shuffled outside. As Tom and his family neared the exit, he overheard the priest introduce himself as Father Joseph Sheehan. He was telling a parishioner that he didn't know how long he would be preaching here. Apparently their regular priest had taken ill and was spending some time in the city. Tom shook hands with Father Sheehan and introduced himself and his family. They welcomed the preacher to the church, complimenting him on a fine sermon.

Tom told the others he wouldn't be home for supper, then mounted his horse and headed for the Connorses farm. He controlled the urge to push his horse into a flat run; he hadn't seen Johnny in what seemed like ages. His old friend hadn't been in church, and Tom hoped he hadn't fallen ill. Johnny was getting on in years, and lately Tom seemed to do nothing but worry about him.

At noon he arrived to find Johnny out back lugging two bags of animal feed. Sunday or not, the animals had to be attended to. Upon seeing him, the old man dropped the bags and rushed over and shook Tom's hand, delighted to have a reason to take a break.

"You weren't at church today."

Johnny squinted at the sky. "No," he said, "I'm getting used to staying home." Taking Tom by the arm, he said, "Come in, come in. Dinner's ready to be served."

Johnny's wife Margaret was standing at the stove taking food from an iron pot, and judging from the smell emanating from the pot, she was a good cook. When they had finished eating, Tom told her as much.

The meal over, Johnny motioned for Tom to go into the parlour for a talk.

A large round table surrounded by four chairs dominated the room. Against the wall opposite the men sat an organ with a matching stool, and nearby, a well-stocked fireplace added warmth and a hearty glow to the place. Tom stepped gingerly across the hardwood floor covered by a large bear pelt.

Johnny said, "Take a seat." This was his practice whenever Tom visited him. He never sat and left a guest standing. The young man pulled one of the smaller chairs out from the table and seated himself, reserving the large stuffed chair at the head of the table for his host.

Grinning, he asked, "Did anyone ever take the big chair?"

Johnny shook his head. "I only ask the people I know to be seated first. I know they won't take my chair."

He took his pipe from his pocket and packed it with tobacco. Coughing once after taking a puff, he asked, "What brought you here today, Tom? You know I can always tell when you have something on your mind. I'm glad you came, though."

Tom told him he had gone to the woods for a week to chop firewood. While there, he said, he'd done a lot of thinking, and soul-searching.

"Johnny, I read the Bible up there every night, until two A.M. once, the very night I had a dream."

He looked out the window and fell silent.

Johnny took his pipe out of his mouth. "Well?" he asked.

"Well what?"

"What was the dream about?"

"Oh," Tom said. With a distant expression on his face he said, "In my dream I was a priest."

Johnny slammed his fist on his knee.

Tom raised his eyebrows and just looked at his friend.

"That's what it was! I couldn't put my finger on it. Sure, that's it! I can see it now. It's written all over you, and I couldn't read it. I think pretty highly of myself when it comes to judging a person, but you had me fooled.

"I can see it now as plain as day," Johnny went on. "You were born to be a priest, a reverend, a clergyman. I never dreamed we'd ever have a priest from around here."

The old man was excited, rocking back and forth in his chair, taking quick, short puffs of his pipe. Finally he laid it down and said with all seriousness, "I'd love to be around to see you then."

"Now, Johnny, I really haven't made up my mind on this, but just in case, I want you to promise not to say a word to Mother or my brothers. I'd want to tell them directly."

"All right, Tom, I promise."

They shook hands and Tom went on his way. He looked back and saw a very proud old man beaming at him. On the way home he pondered the meaning of his dream. Judging from it and his friend's reaction, it certainly seemed as if his path had been laid before him.

Chapter 11

O<small>N THE WAY HOME</small>, Tom reined his horse to a stop as he saw the McCourt vehicle heading toward him. Fred and his daughter Jo came to a stop when they saw it was Tom.

"It's good to see you, Tom," Jo said. "It's been a long time."

That was a half-truth, Tom thought. Indeed, he hadn't seen the young woman in many months, but he doubted the sincerity of her greeting. Jo had blossomed into a beautiful young woman. Her hair fell in long, luxurious tresses to the small of her back. The long and loose blouse she wore only partially disguised her feminine physique. The blouse was unbuttoned a little too far down for Tom's comfort, and just below her throat rested a golden locket suspended from a thin gold chain. Black leather boots travelled up underneath the dress, a tight black belt pinched her narrow waist, and atop her head was a black felt hat.

The two horses pulling their buggy were of the finest breed Tom had ever seen. Each of the noble stallions' legs were covered by white stockings that stood out in stark contrast to their shiny brown coats. They stood alert with their heads held high, their ears pointing forward and their braided tails swaying slightly.

Jo leaned forward and patted one of the horses. "A present from Father for my birthday," she said while looking up at Tom. "Beautiful, don't you think?"

Tom whistled, eyeing the brass and silver buckles harnessing the team. "They sure are."

Jo sat back and said, "I've been away for the past three years, until Father sent for me to come home. He said he had a job for me that paid good money."

Tom was almost afraid to ask. For the first time, Fred spoke. He answered the question nagging at Tom's mind. "Jo will be taking over the Bible class."

Fred examined his fingernails. "We had no one in this area with the qualifications to fill the job. That's why I was forced to call Jo for the job."

Fred lifted his whip and cracked it over the horses, his eyes never leaving Tom. The buggy rumbled past, and when it cleared thirty yards Tom could swear the McCourts were laughing.

At the supper table, William told the family he was going to town later that night. It didn't escape Tom that his oldest brother had been spending a lot of time in O'Neil's Landing ever since the boys had attended a dance a couple of weeks ago. Each of them had danced with a pretty young schoolteacher, but William had swept her off her feet. She was a nice young woman with an easy smile. Her name was Nancy.

Tom asked his brother if he would be seeing Nancy that night. Blushing, William said, "That's right. I've been walking with her for two weeks."

"Good for you," Tom said with a grin. "She's a very pretty girl."

Mary Ann gave William a wary glance. Then she turned to Tom. "Where was Johnny today? I didn't see him at Mass. He isn't sick, is he?"

"No, Mother, he's fine. Mrs. Connors cooked a delicious meal," Tom said, not mentioning the candid talk he'd had with Johnny.

After supper, William left for town and David went outside for a walk. Tom told his mother to stay seated while he cleaned up, but she insisted on helping.

"I met Fred and Jo on the road today," Tom said as he handed a plate to her. "He told me Jo is going to be the new Bible teacher."

Mary Ann said, disgusted, "It seems all they ever do is hurt people. Once, Johnny told me about Fred's father. He was every bit as mean and couldn't get along with anybody. Fred is different, though. Not only is he unpleasant, he goes out of his way to make other people's lives difficult."

When they had finished the dishes, they both sat at the table. "You must have had a hard time after Father died," Tom said suddenly, "with the running of this place, and three small children to care for."

Mary Ann smiled at him. "Yes, Tom, I had to work long, hard hours. Many nights I spent knitting and sewing, making clothes for you three, and clothes to sell to the general store, to keep body and soul together. Many times I wished your father were here."

Mary Ann looked at the old leather chair in the corner, a relic from the days of Tom's grandfather. "All the hard work, the pain and tears, the worry and all the rest of it was worth it. I'd do it all again if given the chance. I'm so very proud of you three."

At Mass, Tom spoke to Johnny about his cabin, a small shack high up in the western mountain range. Tom had gone there with Johnny years ago, when he was fourteen years old. He had never forgotten how quiet and peaceful the area had seemed to him at the time.

Tucked away in a copse of large pines, the cabin sat beside a small mountain stream that provided visitors with cool, fresh water. At night, the only sound was the soft tinkling of water running over pebbles in the stream outside the window. Rich grasslands stretched north and south. Tom regretted that the fields were higher than he'd dare take his cattle in the summertime.

What drew him most of all was the little pool at the south end of the valley. He could close his eyes and see the fish as they leaped from the water, the sun hitting their silvery bodies in a dazzling display. A man could live out there if he wished. Plenty of fish and wildlife and fresh water afforded enough sustenance to last the year round.

While standing outside after the service, Johnny said. "It's been a while since I was out there last, and it looks like I may never be up there again. I'd love nothing better than to be there this very minute, sitting by that pool with my hook in the water and my old pipe going good. But you know, Tom, all good things come to an end, as well as the bad.

"The cabin should be in pretty good shape. You may have to do a little work on it though.

Tom pitied his old friend. The years were finally catching up to him, and he didn't doubt Johnny's saying he'd never get to see the cabin again. A person could only ride so far up the mountain trail, and was then forced to lead the horses up steep footpaths. The going was hard even on young legs, and Johnny's were seventy-seven years old.

"I may be up there for a while," Tom said, "so don't worry if I'm not back in a couple of weeks. I have some thinking to do; I'm sure you know."

"I do, and you're going to the best place on God's green earth to do your thinking." He paused and looked at the ground. When he looked up he said, "Tom, I want you to have that cabin." He looked around to make sure nobody was listening. "It'll be a good place for you to go for relaxation."

"Are you sure?" Tom stammered.

Johnny closed his eyes and nodded. "Yes. I'm sure. I know you will appreciate the place and will keep it up."

This was just too good to be true. Despite his protests, Johnny insisted, and Tom became the proud owner of the modest, but practical cabin.

Tom was truly touched. He shook his friend's hand and went to his carriage. Home, he broke the news to the family.

"Johnny wants me to have his cabin."

Mary Ann was shocked. "Oh my! He gave it to you? There is no end to that man's kindness," she said, shaking her head in disbelief.

"Mother, I'd like to leave tomorrow and spend some time up there."

The day before, William and David had brought the cattle up to their valley, where the animals would graze for the next four months. They weren't expected home until later that evening, and Tom resolved to talk with them when they returned, so he busied himself for the rest of the day with light chores around the farm.

At dusk he sat and read, and within an hour, he heard horses in the yard. Closing his book, he went outside to give his brothers a hand, since they would no doubt be very tired. Tom took the team from them and led the horses to the barn, where he stowed the harnesses away and rubbed down the weary animals, and fed them grain.

When he came inside, his brothers were sitting at the kitchen table wolfing down some beans and potatoes. Mary Ann had come down and was standing at the stove cooking seconds for them. She handed Tom a fresh cup of tea and gestured for him to sit down to join them, bringing a generous platter containing more beans and some fried bread.

While William and David were scraping the last remnants from the platter onto their plates, Tom said to them, "Remember the cabin I told you about? The one Johnny has?"

The boys nodded.

"Well, he gave it to me today."

David groaned. "Really?"

William shrugged. "I can see why. The poor guy probably can't get up there anymore. It's quite a ways up the mountain."

"Anyway," Tom said, "I was thinking about going up there for a week or two. Can you help Mother out while I'm away?"

Looking at their mother and seeing that she didn't object to Tom's plans, they both nodded and went back to eating.

"Take all the time you need," said William.

With an easy mind, Tom prepared for an early departure. He stowed provisions in the saddlebags of the pack horse and tethered his riding horse to the rail. Everything looked to be in order.

Inside, he met his mother in the kitchen cooking breakfast. The smell of freshly made biscuits tempted him to snatch a few from the pan before sitting down. David and William came down and helped themselves to some tea as Mary Ann laid four plates of steaming bacon and eggs on the table.

Tom spoke. "I'll set out after breakfast. It's a long day's travel to Johnny's cabin." Grinning, he corrected himself. "My cabin."

David raised an eyebrow. "Maybe I can use it sometime."

The three followed Tom outside to the horses. The sun crested the eastern horizon and cast scattered patches of light on the porch as it shone through the branches of the sheltering trees.

"This is my favourite time of day," Mary Ann said bemused. "It's just beautiful."

"It's a pretty sight," William agreed, his hands in his pockets.

Untying his horse, Tom asked again, "You're sure it's all right for me to be going on this trip?"

Mary Ann laughed. "Of course, Tom. Get going."

Tom embraced her, and turning to his brothers he said, "Take care of yourselves, and take extra care of Mother."

He mounted the horse and rode off with the pack horse in tow. Mary Ann, William and David waved to him when he looked back, and in a while he and the horses shrank to dots on the horizon.

Mary Ann wondered what was calling Tom out there and wanted to question him about it, but changed her mind. He was a man now, twenty-one on his last birthday, and his reasons were his alone. Whatever it was, she thought, must have been very important for him to want to be away from the farm for so long.

Tom travelled for some time before hunger set in. He figured it to be close to midday, so he slowed the horses to a walk and steered them off the road a way to a grassy clearing near the river. The horses began nibbling the tall grass as he fished around in one of the saddlebags.

He ate some breakfast biscuits and ham washing it down with cool water from the river, not bothering to waste time on a fire for tea. His appetite sated, he took in his surroundings and figured he was an hour from the footpath, where he'd have to dismount and proceed on foot. It would then take four hours of climbing up steep, rocky paths and navigating narrow ledges around dangerous precipices.

Before setting off, he let the horses rest and feed for an hour. Easing himself to a sitting position with his back against a birch tree, he let his mind wander over the many years he had known Johnny Connors. The man was everything Tom had been missing in a father. He had passed on his knowledge of farming, and when the young boys couldn't keep up in the springs and summers, he was there to work alongside them.

His watch showed one-forty, time to be moving on. Setting out at a quick pace, he aimed to make it to the cabin before nightfall.

Within the hour, Tom reached the first steep grade in the foothills. He dismounted and grasped the reins, leading the horses upward. As he walked, he thought of his mother and the hardships she endured keeping the family together.

Their's was a big farm. For generations it had supported just one family, as his father and grandfather had been the only O'Neil children of their generations. The property, he knew, could not support three families. William and David would surely want to stay and work the farm, since they were more suited to the life. Tom possessed an education, but all his knowledge seemed to matter little on their quiet farmstead. Book learning didn't help when it came to tending animals or raising crops.

"I'm the fourth Tom O'Neil," he mused. "And I may be the first to leave the farm."

"We're almost there," Tom said aloud to the horses as they reached level ground. The final stretch would take them through a thick pine forest for two miles. They had made good time and would reach the cabin with plenty to spare.

Half an hour later he broke through the forest and caught sight of Johnny's cabin. Two deer looked up at him from the grassy hillside as he guided the horses up the path. The deer stood stock-still, their eyes glued to him and their noses twitching nervously, before rearing up and darting into the brush.

Tom eased the cabin door open and stepped inside. The stale air assaulted his nose so acutely that he decided to bunk outside under the stars, until the place was aired and dried out.

He ate the remaining few crumbs of the lunch before making a lean-to against one wall. After gathering dry kindling as the sun began to sink toward the distant skyline, Tom lit a fire and placed his small kettle over it to prepare his first cup of tea since breakfast. With a great sigh of satisfaction, he leaned back and took in the night air, allowing it to recharge his body and mind. Tom felt truly at peace, and he only wished Johnny Connors were here to enjoy the solitude.

That night, in a remote area high up on a mountainside, Tom O'Neil IV awoke from a disturbing dream. While the rest of County Armagh slept in the cities and towns and villages below, the young man wrestled in torment with a fast-fading memory.

He had dreamt of Jo McCourt. She had asked him something, to which he had answered, very firmly, "No." The look in her eyes then had been one of purest hate. They were the eyes of the devil. It was a look that promised revenge, but for what, he didn't know.

Chapter 12

MARY ANN CONTINUED her daily chores, but every day Tom was away, she couldn't stop thinking about him. Since his being fired from his teaching, he had thrown himself into farm work with a vengeance. She and the boys were grateful for his contribution, but she knew this was not what he wanted. He worked without complaint and never seemed to tire, yet this life, she felt, was not for him. William and David, it seemed, had been born for farming, but Tom could have more, and she wished she could give it to him.

Mary Ann was lost in thought as William and David came into the kitchen. She placed tea and pie before them both.

David ran a hand through his hair. "There's talk in town about the new school board, and a lot of talk about Jo. Everyone says the fees they paid for Bible studies were a waste. Jo knows nothing about the religious studies, and the word is they want Tom back."

Mary Ann frowned. "As long as Fred is president of the school board, Tom won't be rehired. Besides, I don't think he'd take the job. I don't know what it is, but I believe Tom has something bigger in mind, and when he comes back from his trip he's going to act on it."

"I hope you're right," William said around a mouthful of pie. "I'd rather Tom didn't take the job. Fred and Jo have always had it in for him, and I think taking the position from her would be more trouble than it's worth. Those people are heartless, but worse than that, they're devious." He sighed. "But one of these days the McCourts are going to cross the wrong person."

Mary Ann sipped her tea, deep in thought. She was thinking of her son again. "Maybe," she said.

Tom spent a day patching the cabin roof and insulating the walls. He cleared a small area of rocks and built a crude fence to corral the horses. Until this was finished, they were tethered to stakes positioned near enough to the brook for them to take in water at will. On the third day he would go hunting for venison.

Among the many skills Johnny had taught him was the ability to hunt. Also, the old man had shown him where to preserve the meat once caught. A small opening at the bottom of a square-faced cliff led into a chamber big enough to store several animal carcasses. Ice formed in the little cave year-round. Johnny had kept the meat safe from the elements and predators by enclosing the entrance with two rock slabs.

He went off to hunt and returned with a deer carcass which he stashed in the frigid chamber at the base of the cliff. Making sure his horses were secured in their new corral, he cut the remaining deer into thin strips. He sat back and studied the stars as the mouthwatering aroma of the sizzling meat filled the cool night air.

Tom didn't read that night. Instead, he lay awake in his bunk, deep in thought. What would his father want him to do with his life? He felt sure he wouldn't object to him entering the seminary. In fact, he would most likely have encouraged it.

Many years had passed since the first inkling of priesthood had entered Tom's mind. At ten years old he had felt the slight tug at his heart to preach the Good Word. In the last two years, the feeling had begun to grow and take shape. Now in his twenty-first year, the notion of priesthood had turned into a calling that demanded a firm descision.

Becoming a priest wasn't something a person could take lightly. It was not like becoming a farmer or a teacher, or a miner or even a lumberjack. A man could wear all those hats throughout his life. A priest, on the other hand, shared an unbreakable bond with God, a commitment that, once made, was for life.

Tom was certain his mother would want him to become a priest. She had always been there for him and supported him in all his endeavours. A priest in her family would make her very proud. His brothers treated him as their equal on the farm, but they could see there was something else calling him. He didn't possess the know-how to go into politics or law or business, and teaching and farming didn't speak to him in the same commanding voice as did the Church.

This was the defining moment, the turning point of his existence. He knew what he had to do. When he returned to the farm, he would speak with his mother and brothers and tell them that he wanted with all his heart to become a priest.

Tom's mind was finally put at ease, and he felt the world dropping away from him. He let himself drift away into a deep sleep.

Sunday morning he dressed in a warm woollen sweater against the chilly mountain air and ate a light breakfast outside. He took out his Bible and sat on a nearby log, the same spot where Johnny Connors would sit and read before his age had caught up with him.

Time passed quickly. Two hours later, Tom looked up from the book. It was time to do a little fishing, so shaping a new willow—the one Johnny had made for him long ago was dried and brittle—he walked to the little brook beside the cabin. Silvery fish circled and zigzagged beneath the surface of a pool where the stream's waters collected. He marvelled at how free and wild these creatures were. Fish wanted nothing and asked for nothing. They knew nothing of greed. Johnny had once told him, "The animals on this earth don't need much and want for nothing, whereas man needs far less than he wants."

The old man added, "Human beings are the only species on earth that blush or have reason to blush." Tom knew his words to be true.

One of the fish pulled at the hook, and then the worm was gone. The pool's surface glazed over before his eyes and a vision appeared.

David and William appeared to be no more than six or seven. A much younger version of Mary Ann O'Neil stood beside a dark-haired man who sat with his back against a tree. The man appeared to be in his late twenties, and on his lap rested a Bible. He looked weak, his face a deathly pallor.

The two boys played shirtless beside a sun-dappled pool beneath a swiftly flowing mountain stream. Tom's mother was a beauty to behold, clad in a light summer dress and smiling as though not a care in the world could touch her. She wrapped a blanket around the man, who shivered despite the summer sun and the thick black and red checkered shirt he wore. He looked up at her, pulling his aged face into what looked like a grimace, but what could have been intended as a smile.

His face was very thin. His eyes were glazed as he looked upon the boys, the river, the young woman. He sat as if in constant pain, his body twitching at regular intervals. His lips were a tight pink line whenever he bent to read. Finally, he looked directly at Tom; the pain on his face seemed to melt away in an instant, to be replaced by a look of regret and sorrow.

And then he was gone.

Tom wondered if the man from his vision was his father. He had no living memory of Tom Sr., though the man who sat against the tree bore a striking resemblance to himself. He resolved to ask his mother about the father he never knew and to find out if this vision had been some long-forgotten memory.

Tom remained by the pool an hour longer, his thoughts far away. The first two fish he hooked he released, but he kept the third, a two-pounder. He took it up to the cabin and cleaned it, planning to have it for his supper. He then went outside to the corral and brushed his horses, talking softly to them as night drew on.

Back at the cabin he checked his food supplies. The food he had taken from home, in addition to the deer meat he had stored at the cliff's base, would easily provide for him another week, but he made up his mind to head home before it ran out. Three more days and he would leave, he decided.

Tom shot another deer near the end of the stay. That evening he cooked the hearts and preserved the rest of the meat in the small cave. After dark he found an old shovel that had been used to dig worms, and he recalled Johnny saying that the best time to dig for bait was in the nighttime. Tom hefted the shovel and pried some of the plumpest night crawlers he'd ever seen from the rich soil, then scooped them into a container.

He returned to the cabin and laid his kettle over the fire and then opened a book, as was his practice most nights. When the kettle started to boil, he closed the book and settled down with a cup of tea. For a long time he sat and watched the blue-white moon through the cabin's doorway. A cool breeze blew softly into the cabin, sifting gently through his hair. The only sound came from the murmuring stream outside, punctuated now and again by the breaching of a fish. This was a peaceful place, a good place. Up here, nature's serenity could soothe a man's troubled soul.

In the morning, Tom exited the cabin at first light and opened the corral's gate to let his horses graze. Inside, he fried up some deer meat to go with his tea and the last of his biscuits. When he was done, he washed the pan and cup and placed them on a shelf where Johnny kept his utensils.

Tom looked around the place. Everything appeared to be in order. The repairs of last week had made the cabin habitable for his entire stay, and he was confident they would hold. He took note of the poor state of Johnny's old stove. He reminded himself to bring a replacement for it next time. Tom felt a twinge of sadness as the thought occurred to him that he may not be back for a very long time. Heaving a sigh, he snatched up his fishing rod and went outside to try his luck again at the stream one final time.

It was half an hour later when he put his hook in the water. Within minutes, he pulled six fish from the water. He was confident he could catch more, but Johnny's words on the importance of conservation came back to him. Satisfied with his catch, he carried them back to the cabin.

Tom looked at the stove again and decided he would at least do something to improve its condition. He tied a piece of cowhide over the stovepipe and brushed away some of the dirt that had accumulated since Johnny's last visit. He stepped back and gave it an appraising look. It would have to do. He secured the windows and gathered up his belongings. Closing the door behind him, he walked to the corral and saddled the horses. They seemed almost as eager as he was to start for home.

He mounted the riding horse and headed out through the corral's gate, with the pack horse carrying the deer, in tow. Before he reached the pine thicket, he looked back at the cabin and the surrounding area one last time. Not only was this place his now that Johnny had given it to him, it was *him*. This was where he had confirmed the biggest decision of his life.

"And, God willing, I'll be back," he said, and turned for home.

Tom arrived home late in the afternoon to a warm welcome from his mother. Mary Ann had been out in the garden, and when she first saw him she had dropped her garden spade and sprinted the hundred yards between them to embrace him in a fierce hug.

Tom laughed and hugged his mother back. The two walked beside the horses and back to the barn. On the way he said to his mother, "You have a choice of deer meat or fish for the evening."

Mary Ann smiled. "Fish sounds good to me," she said.

Together they unsaddled the riding horse and removed the saddlebags from the pack horse. Tom slung the deer meat over his shoulder and carried it to the cellar. Inside it was necessary to crouch, until it opened into a low-ceilinged cubicle. The place had been partitioned to separate milk, eggs, berries and fruits, vegetables, and meat.

The place was built to last, the walls made from stone and mortar, the roof from slab rock. The slabs were three and four feet across and three to four inches thick and supported by heavy wooden beams. On top of the slab rock rested four feet of earth that had grown over with a thick sod.

Separate from the cellar was an icehouse, where Tom stored the meat. David and William would bring the ice in by horse and sled from the river in the winter months, and pack it in sawdust.

He returned to the barn and spent the next few hours cleaning and feeding the animals and tidying the loft. William and David walked in just as he was finishing up, and they came over to greet their brother. Tom told them about the work he had done on the cabin, while his brothers filled him in on the goings-on around town in the last two weeks.

They went to the house when their mother called them for supper. Mary Ann said grace after the boys washed up and were seated. When the mountain fish were finished, Tom finished telling his brothers about the trip. He told them about the small brook by the cabin, the corral he had constructed for the horses, and the many deer roaming the area.

"I brought some back and stored it in the icehouse if you want it." The brothers murmured in anticipation of deer meat for their supper tomorrow.

"I have to go tomorrow for a little while to bring some to Johnny. I'm sure he'd like a meal of deer meat, for a change."

When Tom and his mother were alone, he told her of his vision. In it there were two boys that looked like William and David.

"The woman, I think, was you. The man I don't know."

Mary Ann looked at him for a long time before speaking. "What was taking place at the pool?"

"Well, the boys were wrestling and playing and the woman was at the fire with what looked like a kettle in her hand. The man was sitting on the ground, his back against a tree. He had coal-black hair, and in better days he had been a big man. But he seemed cold, and very sick." He didn't tell her that the man sitting by the tree looked very much like him.

Mary Ann continued staring at him. He suddenly felt foolish for having said anything at all. It had been a dream, nothing more.

"Tom, I remember that day like it was yesterday."

Tom gasped.

"It was just a few days before your father died," she went on. "That morning he came down the stairs and told me he wanted to take his boys fishing. He was very weak at the time, and I didn't think he was up to it.

"He surprised me that day. He stayed at the pool watching the three of you play for hours. That night, when he thought he was alone, I heard him pray. 'Thank you, God, for a good day with my wife and the boys,' he said. 'I know I don't have much time left and I understand this is the way it has to be, but that doesn't make it any easier to leave them. I believe in my heart You'll be watching over them.'

"I couldn't see his face in the dark, but I'm sure there were tears in his eyes."

Mary Ann wiped away a tear. "Tom, your father loved us very much. I don't think you had a dream. Your father came to you when you needed him most."

Tom nodded slowly, sudden tears coming into his own eyes. "I have one more question. Which of us boys looks most like him?"

"You do. You're the picture of your father."

The next morning Tom harnessed a team and loaded on the buggy half of the deer meat and the remaining fish in the ice house. He headed for Johnny's place, turning to wave at his mother standing in the doorway as he went.

When he reached the Connorses farm, he went out back and found the old man cleaning out the stables. When Johnny noticed Tom, he came to him and held out his hand.

"Back so soon?"

"I'd have liked to stay longer," Tom replied, "but I did what I went out there to do."

Johnny held up a hand. "Come into the house and tell me everything. If you saw as much as a bee pass the old cabin door, I want to know about that, too."

Tom grinned. "First we have to put your meat away."

"What meat?"

"I shot some deer, and I also brought you a couple of fish."

"From the pool by the cabin?" Johnny asked with a raised eyebrow.

"Yes."

"Wonderful! I was beginning to think I'd had my last meal of brook trout!"

They laughed and put away the meat and fish, then retired to the cozy parlour in Johnny's house. The old man took his favourite chair after Tom seated himself, then lit his pipe. "Now," he said, "start from the beginning and leave out nothing."

Tom began by telling Johnny about the trip to the mountains, describing the stops he had made, the steep grades on the mountainside, even the food he had taken with him. He had almost finished, when the old man held up his hand.

"Time to rest the horses," he said, repacking his pipe. He emptied the cold ashes, then tamped down some more of his sweet-smelling tobacco. He lit the pipe, then gestured at Tom. "It's time to move on."

Tom stared at him a moment, then picked up where he had left off. There wasn't much more to tell, but again he related every detail, from the worms he had dug with Johnny's old shovel, to the cracked stovepipe he had patched with cowhide.

"Oh, I almost forgot, Johnny. I did see a bee or two fly past the door to the cabin."

The old man had been studying Tom's face with great interest. Finally, he spoke up after Tom had finished his story. "Right. You have something more to tell me, so let's have it."

Tom took a deep breath. "I have made up my mind. If I'm accepted, I'll be entering the priesthood this fall."

Johnny stood and took two short steps to Tom. He put his arms around him and hugged him with a strength that belied his age. "Tom, I'm so proud of you! Have you told your mother?"

"No," Tom said, "I wanted you to be the first to know. I'll tell her this evening."

"Tom, I want you to know that I'll help out any way I can."

Tom shook hands with the old man. "Thank you, Johnny," he said. "Thank you so much."

Tom hoped his mother would feel the way Johnny did. If she disapproved, he'd seriously have to re-evaluate his career plan.

William and David weren't at home when Tom opened the door and stepped into the kitchen. He found his mother putting something in the oven. He couldn't tell what it was—some meat dish, he guessed—but it made his mouth water. She straightened and poured a cup of tea for him.

"Tom, sit down and let's have a talk."

Tom sipped his tea while she poured one for herself and sat across from him. Swallowing hard, he reached out and took his mother's hand.

"Mother, I went to Johnny's cabin to spend some time alone and to do some thinking. You know as well as I do this land is too small for all of us. It is good land, but it can only support two families at most."

"What are you getting at? You don't plan on leaving ... do you?"

Tom looked into her eyes. "Yes, Mother, in a way. When I was away, I decided what I want to do. I've known it all along, but my time alone at the cabin was just what I needed to clear my thoughts. What I want to do is join the priesthood. And with your blessing, I will."

Mary Ann gasped. She jumped to her feet and came around the table. She wrapped her arms around her youngest son and said with tears in her eyes, "Tom I'm so proud of you."

"Does this mean I have your permission?"

Mary Ann cried out, "Yes, my son, and God bless you!" Pulling away from Tom, she asked, "Have you told anyone else?"

Tom replied sheepishly, "You must forgive me, Mother. I wanted to tell Johnny first. I wanted to get his reaction."

"What was it?"

"About the same as yours."

Mary Ann laughed. "Good," she said.

"Then you're not mad at me for not telling you first?"

"Tom, have you ever known me to be mad at you or your brothers?"

Tom thought for a moment. "No, Mother. Never." He looked around. "When will they be back, anyway?"

"After you left for Johnny's, they went to the valley to check on the herd." She looked at the clock on the wall. "If I leave now I should be able to catch them. If it's all right with you, I'd like to talk to them about their little brother wanting to be a priest." She grinned.

"Of course, Mother."

Mary Ann was bubbling with excitement. "Will you help me get ready? It's been a long time since I took a ride. It'll do a world of good to sleep under the stars."

"What horse will you be taking?"

"The grey," Mary Ann said.

Tom went out to the barn and came back leading the grey mare with one hand and carrying a saddle in the other. Mary Ann came to the door just as he saddled up the horse. She was dressed to ride and had a cloth bag of provisions.

Tom smiled at her and said, "You be careful."

She mounted and kicked the horse into motion. The mare needed little urging and headed down the dusty road. Tom watched her until she had faded from view, then went inside to finish his tea. He cleaned and washed his dishes, then busied himself around the barn. He cleaned the stalls and fed the stock, before taking up a broken harness to mend.

Night fell, and Tom went inside to read by candlelight. He was reading the Book of Matthew when he looked up and suddenly realized that this would be the first night he had ever spent alone in the house. It reminded him pleasantly of his solitude up at Johnny's cabin.

Chapter 13

MARY ANN RODE HARD to meet her sons at the valley. She thinking of money. The family could not afford to send Tom to the seminary at this time, but she didn't let this discourage her. He was an honourable young man who had a noble goal, and if she would have to work harder and longer hours for the next few years to make his dream a reality, then so be it.

She was a woman of great faith. Since the day her husband had told her Grandfather's advice, she had put her life in God's hands and left it there. Thinking back, Mary Ann could not recall ever having been in want for food, warmth or a place to live. For this she uttered a silent prayer of thanks as she rode on beneath the darkening sky.

William hunkered down to start a campfire for his and David's supper. He heard a noise off to the left, and he stood to investigate. Coming up the trail was a horse he thought looked familiar. It came closer, and he was alarmed to see the rider was his mother.

She held up her hand. "Hi, William."

"What is it, Mother? What's happened?"

"Relax, William, nothing's the matter. I just rode out here to get some exercise." At William's questioning look, she said, "All right, I want to talk to you two about something."

"It must be pretty important to ride all the way here."

"You'll know after we have had our supper. I want David to hear it too. Don't worry, I have good news."

William helped his mother down from the horse and guided her to a comfortable spot near the fire. He handed her a tin plate of meat and leftover biscuits from breakfast. She sat and ate in silence, waiting for David. When he emerged from the woods carrying an armload of kindling, he saw his mother, and immediately a puzzled expression crossed his face, but a look at William reassured him.

They waited patiently for Mary Ann to finish her tea. When she drained the last few drops, William was quick off the mark. "What's on your mind, Mother?"

"I have news about Tom. You know he's been a voracious reader, and a great scholar on biblical matters. Well, he wants to become a priest."

William was astonished. "Are you sure?" he managed to get out.

"It's true. He just told me," Mary Ann said. "I came out here so we could talk this over among ourselves. I'm all for it, myself, and told him so."

"If anyone can become a priest, Tom can," William added.

With the coming dawn, the trio rode home in high spirits.

Tom woke up early and went outside. Maintaining a farm was also a lifetime commitment, he mused. Chores could never go undone, else the farm fall into disrepair. Animals had to be fed, stalls to be cleaned, water to be drawn. Firewood had to be stocked, hay to be hewn, vegetables had to be set, fertilized, weeded and harvested. It was a demanding life. When the sun was an hour in the sky he went inside to fix a hearty breakfast. He fried a thick slice of smoked ham and two eggs, and piled on a generous serving of biscuits.

He planned to meet with Father Sheehan in O'Neil's Landing, and set out by horse. He would first try the priest's home, and if he wasn't there, the church. While riding, he came alongside Johnny's place and decided to visit.

Johnny was out front, as if he had been expecting someone. "You're all dressed up this morning," he noted as Tom pulled into the yard.

"I'm on my way to town and was wondering if you'd like to come along."

Johnny pushed his fingers through his snow-white hair and nodded. "Yes, I'd love to tag along."

They talked about the weather as they travelled. The crops in O'Neil's Landing had been experiencing a good run of weather this year. "This has been a good year for all things," Johnny mused.

"Johnny, can I ask you a question?"

"Sure, ask me anything you want."

"If you had life to live over again, would you do anything differently?"

"First of all, I don't have life to live over again. Secondly, there isn't one thing I'd change. Tom, I believe you're put on this earth to do your lot and for a certain length of time, and when your work is done the Lord will take you home."

"Is that what happened to my father? He was so young when he died."

Johnny gave the young man an appraising look. "Yes. Your father's work was finished and he was called home. I'm seventy-seven years old, but my work and purpose isn't completed. Do you believe you're here for a reason? Do you believe your two brothers are here for farming, and that you were put on this earth for preaching?"

"Yes, Johnny, I do."

They had reached the town. Tom asked Johnny to wait for him.

"I think I'll go visit Billy Nolan while you take care of your business. I haven't seen him in a while, and I'm sure he has a few good stories to tell me." Grinning, he added, "And most will be lies."

Tom laughed. "All right, where is he?"

"That old crook will be at the general store, listening to all the gossip."

Johnny made his way to the general store, and dismounted just as Billy Nolan was coming through the door. He caught sight of Johnny and rushed up to help him down. "You're not as spry as you used to be," he said, teasingly. Tom flicked his horse's reins and was about to tell Johnny he'd be back later, but the two old friends were already trading taunts and matching lie for lie.

At the other end of town, Tom stopped his horse beside a newly painted picket fence before Father Sheehan's small, single-storey house. He dismounted and climbed the three steps leading to the front door, where he nervously rapped, using the big brass knocker. The lady who answered was a dark-complexioned woman in her mid-fifties.

"My name is Tom O'Neil, and I'd like to speak with Father Sheehan. However, I don't have an appointment."

"That's fine," the housekeeper said. "He's free at the moment. Please, step inside."

Tom entered the house and looked around. Though it was small house, it was comfortable, with plush, colourful rugs on the sparkling hardwood floor. The finest of handcrafted furniture was here, its mahogany burnished to a shine. Fresh-picked flowers stood in tiny, delicate vases. Tom was still staring in awe when the woman came back into the foyer and said, "You may go in now. Father Sheehan will see you."

She led him down a hallway to a small room whose lone occupant sat behind a desk. Thanking the woman, Tom walked in and said, "Good day, Father. I hope I'm not interrupting anything."

"Oh, no," the priest said, removing his spectacles and placing them on the desk before him. "It's a pleasure to see you again. Please sit down. Is there something I can help you with?"

"I hope so," Tom said as he took a seat. "I'm not sure of the process, but I want to enter the priesthood."

"When I woke this morning I wondered what surprises God had for me today. This is wonderful. I know your family, so I wouldn't anticipate any problems. I'll do what I can to place you in the seminary this coming fall." He called for his housekeeper. When she came to the door, he asked her to bring him and his guest some tea.

"I understand you're quite a knowledgeable young man," the priest resumed. "And, from what I've heard, you were quite the teacher. It is only natural that you would want to be a priest."

They talked for a little over an hour. In that time, Tom told the priest about his upbringing on the small farm. He said he had always known somehow that the life of a priest is the life he wanted. Dedication and hard work were his food and drink. The priest listened intently as Tom told him of his background: the founding of O'Neil's Landing by his great-great-grandfather

William O'Neil; the untimely death of his father; his mother's perseverence.

Outside, Tom shook the priest's hand.

"I'll write the Bishop immediately. He's a very busy man, but hopefully we'll hear from him within two weeks."

Tom smiled. He felt he had found a good friend in this man. Thanking him for his time, Tom put on his hat and mounted his horse.

At the general store, Johnny Connors and Billy were laughing and appeared to have settled their differences. Johnny spotted the horse, and bade farewell to his friend. The two rode home with a light wind blowing from the southwest, Johnny smoking his pipe in silence and Tom deep in thought about the coming weeks.

Chapter 14

For THE NEXT TWO WEEKS, Tom grew more and more anxious; he was working too hard but couldn't help it. During this time, Johnny Connors stopped by, came into the barn, and saw him working feverishly, stacking hay. "Tom, you're overexerting yourself."

"I'm just having a really busy week, Johnny."

"Tom, I can always tell when there's something on your mind. Do you want to tell an old friend?"

Tom straightened and wiped his brow. "Johnny," he said, "I can't stand all this waiting. When we went to town the other day, I spoke with Father Sheehan about the priesthood, and I still haven't heard any word from the Bishop. I guess patience is one thing I'm going to have to learn. I keep praying for the days to pass quicker, and I'm trying to keep myself occupied with work."

A broad smile crossed Johnny's face. "Well, my boy, I'm delighted you took that important step. I know just what you need."

"What?"

"A day fishing."

Tom burst out laughing. Fishing had been the last thing on his mind. But seeing Johnny with that big grin gave pause to his anxiety. "Why not? You be here bright and early tomorrow morning."

Johnny winked. "I'll be here," he said.

The next day, Johnny walked into the kitchen to find Tom fixing breakfast for the two of them.

"Looks like it's going to be a good one," the old man remarked. He sat and hummed a tune while Tom cooked. He stopped in the middle of the second verse when something occurred to him.

"Tom, did you know Fred McCourt had to make a trip to the city?"

"No," Tom said, filling the teapot. "Should I have heard?"

"Well, no, I suppose. I heard his girl ... what's her name?"

"Josephine is her name ... Jo."

"Yes," Johnny said, "Jo, that's it. The word is she got married to some fellow. They say he's a rich merchant, but I doubt he will be for very long."

"But Johnny, she can't take anything from him, can she?"

"Of this girl, I know very little. But Fred knows how to get what he wants and he doesn't care who he tramples on to get it. You heard what the McCourts did to that young girl back some years ago."

"I never did hear the full story."

Johnny shook his head in wonder. "The poor girl couldn't have been more than fifteen years old at the time. Fred, I believe, was sixteen. She was out in the field alone when Fred came riding by. He wanted his way with her, but she turned him down, not aware the McCourts didn't take no for answer. Well, he raped her.

"She managed to get to town and tell the law, but the man in charge was a real good friend of Fred's parents. Friend is too strong a word. Fred's old man James owned the lawman and he could have had him sacked at a moment's notice.

"I was in the courthouse the day of the trial. The place was packed solid. Fred came in with a well-dressed lawyer named Stephen Rourke, one of the best in the country. The judge was also a relative of Fred's mother.

"Rourke accused her of making up the charge just so her family could get their hands on the McCourt money. He called her down into the dirt, with the poor girl's parents watching from the crowd.

"The jury had no choice but to find him not guilty. After all, he was from a family of good social standing. When it was over, the McCourts retaliated with a lawsuit against her for damaging Fred's good name. The family settled out of court by giving over their land."

Tom whistled. "It's hard to believe that one person would do a thing like that to another."

"I told you before and I'm telling you now. You can never let your guard down when it comes to the McCourts."

It was still early in the morning by the time they reached the fishing hole. This would likely be the last time they would ever go fishing together, Johnny thought.

That night, a letter from Father Sheehan was waiting for Tom. His heart leapt in his throat when his mother handed it over. The priest wrote, "Tom, I want to talk to you on Sunday morning before Mass at the church."

For the next two days Tom didn't stop. He worked hard at everything he could find. He was scared, and he didn't even realize it until the second day, when his mother said to him, "Tom, you're not thinking straight. If you don't get into the seminary this year, don't lose faith. God has His reasons for everything. You're worrying for nothing."

Tom sighed. "Yes, you're right, Mother. However things turn out Sunday will be the way they should be."

Sunday morning Tom got up and cooked breakfast so it was waiting by the time everyone else awoke. When Mary Ann came into the kitchen, she looked him up and down and smiled.

Tom looked at the wall clock. He had to leave soon to talk with the priest. "I'll ride one of the saddle horses," he said, "and you three can come later by buggy."

William laughed. "Not a chance! We want to be there to congratulate you when he says you're going to the seminary."

Father Sheehan was the only person in the church when they arrived. Mary Ann and William and David waited at the back of the church while Tom walked up the centre aisle to meet the priest. They said a few words, then Tom waved to his family to come closer.

The clergyman's face was a stone mask. Mary Ann looked from him to her son, wondering what had happened. She had a bad feeling about this. She was about to lay a comforting hand on her son's shoulder, when Father Sheehan cleared his throat.

He turned to Tom. "Congratulations," he said, his face breaking into a smile. "You have been accepted for college. Now, I know you're sure of your decision, but I have to ask so that the Bishop knows. Do you have any doubts?"

Tom shook his head at once. "No, Father, I want this more than anything."

Father Sheehan shook Tom's hand and said, "I somehow know you'll do what you set out to do."

He then turned to Tom's mother. "I'm new here, Mrs. O'Neil, and your sons were men before I came. But I've heard stories of how hard you worked to raise your boys and run your farm. The people of the congregation speak very highly of you."

Turning once again to Tom, he said, "If I can be of any help to you now or in the future, don't hesitate to ask."

When Mass was over, Father Joseph Sheehan informed the churchgoers of the news, and asked them all to pray for Tom's success. Further, he implored the members of the congregation to help Tom any way they could.

Outside, Johnny and Tom met on the steps. "Words can't say how happy I am for you," he said, and placed an envelope in Tom's hand. "I've been wanting to give you this since the day you confided in me. I want to help you through college, and God willing, I'll live long enough to see you come home wearing your collar."

Tom didn't open the envelope until that evening at the supper table. He looked inside, then around the table at his family. He withdrew a folded piece of paper and read aloud to his family "Tom, just a little to help you in some way, and may God bless you. Your old friend, Johnny."

He looked in the envelope again and withdrew a wad of bills. William and David looked at each other in amazement, but Mary Ann just watched Tom count the money.

"There's a hundred pounds here."

Chapter 15

OVER THE NEXT THREE DAYS, the O'Neils' friends dropped by to wish Tom well. Some were even kind enough to contribute money. He still felt uneasy about Johnny's extremely generous contribution, but he couldn't convince him to take the money back.

Tom also didn't like the thought of straining the family's finances. They had already sacrificed much, and to ask for more would be selfish. He said this to his mother as the last guests filed out Wednesday evening.

Mary Ann was firm. "Tom, we don't want you to say or even think it. Your brothers and I have talked this over and we've agreed to do everything in our power to make sure you get your education. Now," she said with a note of finality, "don't say any more on it."

William spoke. "Tom, don't worry so much. We'll come up with the money to cover expenses."

"Yeah," David added with a wink, "we won't steal it."

Tom spent the rest of the week preparing for the trip. Mary Ann planned to take him to the train station by horse and buggy, on the pretense of visiting some friends.

Mary Ann felt more and more depressed the closer the day of Tom's departure came. She awoke on the big day with a sad acceptance in her heart. Her baby boy was going away and the most she could expect to hear from him would be through long-distance correspondence. Heaving a sigh, she dressed and went downstairs to make breakfast.

When the boys came down, Mary Ann said, "Tom, you sit and eat your breakfast. William and David will hitch the horses to the buggy and bring it to the front of the house."

While he was eating, the baggage was lashed to the buggy. A warm wind blew from the southwest, more like July than the seventh of September. Tom looked to the north toward the swiftly flowing river, recording the distant crash of the waterfall. Shielding his eyes against the sun, he surveyed the land before him that had served as his home for more than twenty years.

If I had been cut out to be a farmer, he thought, *I wouldn't want to be anywhere else.*

"You'll do well with this place," he said to his brothers. He took both their hands and said, "Look after each other."

Mary Ann was sitting aboard the buggy, a slightly pained expression on her face. Tom stepped on board and sat next to her. She flicked the reins and the horses clattered down the path.

On the main road, as they passed Johnny's farm, Tom spoke. "Will I ever see him again?"

"God willing."

Mary Ann brooded in silence about Tom's leaving as they rode. She worried more about his future than she did his brothers'. William and David were strong young men who could make a comfortable living at farming, but Tom was setting off on an unknown adventure to discover his true lot in life.

As they passed the river, Tom stretched and let out a yawn.

"See those rocks circling that pile of ashes? It looks like a good place to stop and make a cooking fire."

Mary Ann looked back. "Yes," she said, "that will give the horses time to graze."

Tom fetched a kettle full of water from the stream while Mary Ann rummaged for some food.

As they waited for the water to boil, Mary Ann said, "Tom, your father would be so proud of you. He had great respect for priests."

They reached the railroad station one hour before the train was to arrive. They waited without talking, Mary Ann stealing occasional glances at Tom, wondering when she would see him again. Tom fidgeted nervously with his luggage and checked his pocket watch every few minutes.

When the train whistle blew, a feeling of loneliness came over Tom. He was leaving the only home he had ever known.

The conductor's voice cut through the air. "All aboard!"

Tom embraced his mother and kissed her cheek. "I love you, Mother," he said.

"I love you too, my son," Mary Ann said, her voice cracking. Tom touched her face and wiped away a tear.

"You be careful and come back safe."

Tom hefted his carrying bag and walked toward the train. He stopped for a moment and turned. "I'll write when I can," he said, then turned slowly and stepped aboard.

Inside the coach, Tom looked around for an empty seat. He removed his coat and hat, placed them on the seat nearest the window, and took his place in the aisle seat facing the front of the train. Seated across from him were two men embroiled in what looked like a game of poker. They were passing back and forth a bottle of liquor.

One of the men invited Tom to have a drink. He declined the offer and instead leaned back in his seat and closed his eyes. Johnny had told him once that all the O'Neil men would take a drink now and then, but the old man had never seen any of them drunk. One day Tom had found a bottle of corn whiskey lying in the hayloft. He had taken the cork from the bottle and downed a mouthful. He nearly choked on the vile liquid, but curiosity got the better of him and he took another swallow. He must have drained the whole bottle, because his next conscious thought was waking next to his mother, asleep in a chair beside him. He had a splitting headache and his stomach was churning.

It had taken quite some time to recover from that bout with alcohol. He was sixteen years old at the time. He later learned William had brought it home from town and had hidden it from their mother. It was the last time Tom touched liquor.

His thoughts were disturbed by loud angry voices. He opened his eyes to see the two men on their feet taking swings at each other. They were cursing and spitting, and Tom glanced at the table at which they had been sitting. The bottle was empty. *Some people*, he thought, *the bottle changes them completely*. Taking his coat and hat, he moved to the other end of the coach.

The noise in the back of the coach grew to a crescendo. Suddenly the door at the front opened and two big men came in carrying billy clubs. He didn't bother looking back as the policemen moved toward the rear of the car. Two sharp cracks resounded, and the arguing ceased.

Tom tried to rest, but sleep would not come. He gazed out the window at the blue-black sky and reminisced on the life he was leaving behind. A full moon hid behind thick scudding clouds, and the shadows of landmarks flew past the train. He fell asleep, and the next thing he knew, a conductor had come through the door, announcing that breakfast was being served.

Tom decided to try his luck, hoping the dining car wasn't full. Taking the nearest table, he sat facing the front and picked up the menu. The prices made him feel uneasy, but the choice of steak or ham, with two eggs and fried potatoes, made his mouth water. He made his choice and laid down his menu.

The waiter brought tea just as the two card players from the night before came in and sat at a nearby table. They appeared to have sobered up considerably, though Tom suspected their encounter with the authorities had more than a little to do with that. He overheard one say he couldn't recall any of last night's events. The other complained of a very bad headache. Tom grinned despite himself, recalling the headache William's corn whiskey had given him.

As he ate, Tom noticed out of the corner of his eye a young woman watching him with great interest. She turned to the window view when Tom didn't return her gaze. Moments later, he saw her speaking to an older lady, who might have been her mother. The young woman looked again his way, but this time there was no smile on her face. Tom imagined he saw a flash of anger in her eyes.

The end of the line was in a town unknown to him. He retrieved his luggage and sought out the nearest hotel, where he asked for directions to the seminary. The next morning, he hired a horse-drawn coach to take him to his new home.

The seminary complex was located in a remote area surrounded by mountains. Two enormous stone buildings stood in defiance to the surrounding landscape. One of the buildings he guessed was the school, the other a residence for students. As the coach neared the site, Tom saw a cluster of small houses, a barn and corral, and a low, flat-roofed building that had to be an outhouse. Standing apart from the other buildings was a modest-sized church.

Tom was met at the entrance of the school by a man who appeared to be in his mid-fifties. He welcomed the new student and beckoned. "Follow me."

Tom grabbed one of his trunks and had to hurry to keep pace with the older man. He was led to the entrance of one of the stone buildings, and up a short flight of stairs to a long, narrow hallway with doors on either side.

"Here is where you'll be sleeping," the man said matter-of-factly. Opening the first door, he introduced Tom to Robert Green, his roommate, who had arrived the day before. Tom held out his hand and said, "Tom O'Neil. Pleased to meet you, Robert."

"Welcome."

The first thing to catch Tom's eye was the tiny window at the back of the room, which was covered by vertical steel bars. There were two beds, one on either side of the room, and next to each bed was a small chest of drawers and a writing table. From an iron ring in the ceiling hung a heavy oil lamp.

"You see how this room is now?" the instructor said.

"Yes," Tom replied.

"This is the way I want it to be at all times when you aren't in your beds. You'll receive your orders on that later. Now, come. I'll show you where you'll get your meals."

He gathered together other arrivals, and led them downstairs into a large, plain dining room. Tall wooden stools sat behind long wooden tables spanning the length of the room. The instructor led them to a counter that ran along one wall.

"This is where you'll pick up your meal, and you'll always sit in the same spot at this table. When finished, take the plate, mug and utensils over here." He pointed. "You'll leave any leftover food there, although," he added with what Tom thought was a smirk, "I doubt there'll be any waste."

He drew up straight. "That about covers it. Oh, yes," he said, "in bed by nine, all lights out, and up at six."

When Robert closed the door to their room behind him, he shook his head and said to Tom, "This isn't going to be a picnic."

"We'll have to see. How about showing me around the grounds?"

Robert agreed, and the two left their sleeping quarters to explore the outbuildings. First they went to the church, which seemed even smaller from the inside. But then, he thought, this was a small campus, whose staff was comprised of only half a dozen instructors. He had no idea how many students were in residence.

After satisfying his curiosity about the place, Tom and Robert returned to their dormitory. They were met at the front door by an old man, a caretaker, Tom reasoned.

"You'd better get back to your room," he advised. "It'll soon be mealtime."

Tom was inspecting the meagre lodgings more thoroughly when a bell rang, signalling suppertime. He got in line at the counter, and when he reached the serving area, he was surprised to be handed a tray containing a small plate of beans, a slice of bread, and a mug filled with tea.

The server noticed Tom's hesitation and said, "No seconds."

Tom again examined the contents of his tray and turned to walk toward the stool that would be his for the next several years. This was a test, he surmised as he sat down. He didn't know how long the others would be expected to live on such a diet, but it mattered little to him. He was up to the challenge.

Back in their room, Robert said to him, "What did you think of our supper?"

Tom grinned. "The beans tasted good."

He had made up his mind to be a priest, and not complain of personal sacrifice. If it meant he'd have to go hungry, so be it. He would achieve his goal.

Chapter 16

TOM AND ROBERT WERE among a class of twenty new students, some more enthusiastic than others. Not all of them would graduate. The rigours of training for the priesthood taxed not only the body, but also one's mind and spirit. Tom had no problem adjusting to this structured lifestyle; in his mind, he knew the journey would make the reward that much sweeter.

While Tom was exploring the little church one day, the caretaker he had met the first day approached him.

"You're the fellow they call O'Neil," the caretaker stated.

"Yes, I'm Tom O'Neil," he said.

The caretaker laughed. "This coming spring I will have worked here forty years. I came here to study for the priesthood long ago, but I was one of fifteen in a class of twenty who didn't make the grade. That fellow rooming with you, he ..." The old man stopped and shook his head. "I don't know about him; he doesn't belong here. But you, Tom, you're cut from the right stuff."

Tom didn't comment, but secretly he agreed with the caretaker's appraisal of his roommate.

The seminary was an old institution that dated over three hundred years. It was rumoured that of every twenty who entered, only five became priests. Tom believed it. After only two months, three students had dropped out.

Robert was having a hard time. Many nights Tom would hear him talk in his sleep. He liked the fellow, and wished there were something he could do to help his friend adjust to life at the seminary. One night, after Robert's nocturnal ramblings grew particularly loud, Tom woke him up.

He leaned up on one elbow, sure he could hear his roommate crying. Tom spoke lowly. "Robert, are you sleeping?"

A minute passed with no reply, and Tom eased himself back down on the bed.

"No," said Robert finally.

Tom threw back his covers and crossed the room to Robert's chair.

"Do you want to talk about it?"

There was a long silence. It dragged on interminably, and Tom thought his friend had at last fallen asleep. He stood and turned to his own bed when Robert's voice drifted up.

"Don't go. I need to talk to someone I trust."

Slowly he removed his covers and sat on the edge of the bed. In the moonlight Tom could see him wiping moisture from his eyes.

"I come from a very rich family," Robert began. "The money came from my mother's side. I love my mother very much, but she's a very demanding person when she wants to be. From the time I was ten years old, she'd been making plans for me to become a priest.

"There's a girl back home whom I love very much, and she loves me. We both want to get married and start a family, and to make our own way in life. I don't want to be a priest. I never did, and I never will."

Tom laid a comforting hand on his friend's shoulder. "Here's what you should do. Write your mother; tell her how you feel. Tell her you want to marry this girl and that you don't want to become a priest. If she doesn't accept your decision now, she will in time."

"I wish it were that easy. She'd never understand! It would break her heart to have her lifelong dream shattered. Tom, you're a good friend and in time, you'll walk from this place with your collar. You were made for the priesthood. But Tom, my friend, I feel trapped."

"Robert, I know you're troubled by this. Don't you think your mother would put your happiness ahead of her own?"

"You'd have to know her. She wouldn't." Robert seemed to relax a little. It seemed the talk, though it hadn't resolved the dilemma, settled him down, and Tom returned to bed.

Trap. The word resounded from somewhere within Tom's memory. Where had he heard it before? A sense of foreboding washed over him as he struggled to remember who had said it. No good had come of it, of that he was sure. He returned to his bed and lay awake for a long time, praying his friend would make the right decision. Sleep didn't come easy for either of them that night.

On December 22, Tom received a parcel from home. His mother had sent him some warm clothing for the coming winter, a cake sealed in a box, two bottles of homemade jam, and a letter. Tom read the letter twice before laying it down. A passerby in the dorm hallway might have garnered from the look on his face that Tom was feeling homesick. Letting out a small sigh, he opened the box and took a nibble of his mother's cake.

Across the room, Robert sat on his bed, busily unwrapping a large package. He took one look inside the oversized box and shook his head in disgust.

"Look at this," he said, emptying the contents onto the bed. A gold pocket watch, two silk shirts, and three pieces of silver cutlery tumbled out. There was no letter.

Waving a hand at the ostentatious display, Robert said, "I don't want any of these things. She'll never give me what I want."

"What would that be?" Tom asked. He already knew the answer.

"Permission to leave this school and live my own life."

Tom had stood up and crossed the room in two quick steps before Robert had finished. "Listen," he said. "Pack your things and leave. Your mother will learn to accept it."

Robert looked up at him and blinked. For a moment he looked as if he'd gathered the strength to defy his mother. Then his shoulders slumped, and defeated, he looked at the floor.

Tom was at a loss. The priest who was his spiritual supervisor had been of little help when Tom had asked for advice on Robert's predicament. He had said pretty much what Tom had expected. "Some are born for the priesthood. It is not something that can be learned, or wished upon anyone."

He took out a textbook and began reading, occasionally lifting his eyes from the page to look at Robert. At one point Tom caught him stealing glances at his own letter from O'Neil's Landing. Perhaps reading the letter from Tom's mother might help him realize that a better life awaited him outside the seminary, a life that included a family.

Tom never knew what the word lonesome meant until the night of Christmas Eve. Robert lay on his bed not saying a word. He hadn't said much at all the last few days, and it wasn't helping Tom's loneliness. He pictured David and William sitting around the kitchen table at the farmhouse, rubbing their hands in anticipation of the feast their mother would be preparing for Christmas Day. Then there was the empty chair at the table ...

Tom had to force himself to stop thinking like this.

Robert's voice carried to his side of the room. "You're missing your family. It's written all over your face." Tom sat up on his bed and peered at his friend.

Robert continued. "My family is not close. We hardly ever get together on Christmas, since my mother is always away. She has more important things to do with her bigshot friends, I suppose. Most times I'd be left home alone with the maid.

"All I ever wanted was for her to spend Christmas at home with me. Tom, you're lonely because you're not home tonight, but I'm twenty-two years old and I've been feeling this way every night."

"Robert, I'm so sorry." He hadn't realized how lucky he was to have a family who loved him. Without that, he thought, he would truly be lost.

In the first class after the holiday season, the teacher announced that the Bishop would be paying them a visit and would address each class individually over the next few weeks.

"Those of you who finish your training will become very familiar with this man."

Robert seemed to gradually rise from his depression. He began to talk more, sometimes excitedly. Tom hadn't seen him this happy all year. He even noticed Robert writing sometimes at night, and Tom supposed his friend was finally taking a stand against his overbearing mother.

One evening, as the mealtime bell rang, Robert looked up from his notes and told Tom to go on ahead. "I'll be right down. I have a few more lines to write."

Tom entered the dining room and took his seat with tray in hand. He had grown accustomed to the students' modest meals by now. The first week of school had required some adjusting to eating these minute amounts, but after that he didn't mind at all. Robert, he recalled, had always found something to complain about, from the scant food to the long hours of study their training demanded. But his friend seemed to be taking some initiative in his life now. Tom silently congratulated him.

Tom finished his supper, but lingered over his cup of tea so Robert wouldn't have to eat alone when he came down. Ten minutes later he drained the last few drops from his cup. Pushing back his stool, he stood and returned his tray to the counter before heading upstairs to see what was keeping his friend.

He knocked, and pushed the door open. Tom's knees buckled as he fell to the floor, choking a scream that threatened to come out. Straight ahead was Robert Green hanging by the neck. A leather belt was looped through the ceiling's lamp hook.

Robert's arms hung limp at his sides, his shoulders pulled down in one final gesture of defeat. His eyes bulged sightless in their sockets, and his cheeks bore an unsightly purple cast.

Trapped. The word struck him solidly, like a slap across the face. He remembered now. His mother had once told him about

Sheilagh McCourt's unfortunate demise. Living with Fred had made her feel like a caged animal. She had taken the only way out she knew, and now so had Robert.

Tom clutched his stomach, but he couldn't hold his supper down. Panic enveloped him, and he knew he had to get out of there. He scrambled to his feet and rushed out of the room, making his way to the emergency bell.

Soon the hall crowded with students, teachers, caretakers and servants eager to see who was sounding the alarm. One of Tom's teachers pushed his way through the crowd. "What is it? Is there a fire?"

"There's no fire," Tom said, grief-stricken.

Bishop Brown joined the group. "Why did you ring the bell?"

There was no easy way to say it, so he just came out with it. "Robert Green hanged himself."

His teacher frowned. "What did you say?"

Tom pointed toward his room and repeated himself. "Robert Green hanged himself. He's dead."

Bishop Brown issued sharp commands for the assembled crowd to back away from Tom's room. He went inside the room briefly, then came out closing the door behind him. "Go notify the police," he said to the caretaker. "The rest of you, to the dining room. Now!"

Tom followed the students downstairs. Shortly, the Bishop entered and asked who had discovered the body. Tom slowly raised his hand.

"All right, son, you'll have to come with me. The authorities will want to question you."

Tom spoke up. "We're not going to leave him there like that, are we?" The nearest police station was an hour away. The thought of his friend left hanging from a hook in his room chilled him.

"We shouldn't touch anything," the Bishop asserted.

"But what harm will it do to let him down? We can lay him on the floor."

The Bishop turned to the caretaker and ordered him to lock the door and to let no one in there. He then turned to Tom and said, "We'll find another room for you to sleep in tonight."

Sleep was the furthest thing from Tom's mind, but he didn't argue.

When the police arrived, they went straight to the scene of the hanging. Two officers went in and closed the door behind them, while a third stood guard outside. When the officers came out of the room, the taller of the two went to Bishop Brown and said, "There's no need for further investigation, but I would like to talk to the person who found him."

The Bishop and the officer went to the dining room and sought out Tom at his table. The young man was staring straight ahead, the cup of tea in front of him untouched. The officer took the seat opposite him and said, "I'd like to ask you a few questions. This won't take long, son."

Tom looked up.

"We found several letters. One was addressed to a Mrs. Elizabeth Green, and another to the law. In the note to us, he clearly stated that you are not to be suspected of any involvement in the matter of his death, that it was all his own doing. Here's the envelope addressed to you."

Tom looked at the envelope, then back at the officer. He opened it and read in a shaky voice, "To Tom O'Neil, the best friend I have ever known. To you I leave all the things at this seminary belonging to me, Robert Green. I'm sorry if my passing has caused you any trouble; I'm also sorry I will not be here to shake your hand when you're ordained in the priesthood. Goodbye, Tom, and God Bless. Robert Green."

A moment passed in silence before the officer cleared his throat. "Tom, we are satisfied there was no foul play in the death of your friend. We are curious, though, why a young man such as Robert Green would want to kill himself. He seemed to have everything going for him."

"Robert was unhappy," Tom said. "His mother wanted him to become a priest more than anything. He told me not long ago that he had never wanted to become one. He had a girl waiting for him back home.

"Why was he here, then?" the officer asked.

"I asked him the same question."

"And?"

"To please his mother."

"I see."

The officer took the letter back from Tom, glanced at it, then asked, "And what is it you have that he didn't?"

Tom took a moment to answer. His eyes were drawn to the Bishop, who had been watching and listening quietly. Slowly he said, "Robert's parents are wealthy people. He had all the material things anyone could ever want, but the thing he wanted most can't be bought. What he wanted was to feel needed and loved by his family."

The officer stood up. "All right. I think we're about done here."

Tom and Bishop Brown followed the officer outside. They walked to the police wagon, in the back of which lay Robert Green's body wrapped in a tarp. Tom said a little prayer for his friend's soul, then blessed himself.

"What a waste of life," he said softly.

The officer nodded. "Sure is."

A few days after the tragedy, classes resumed at the seminary. Many of the students were still in shock over the sudden death of one of their own, but the teachers would not let them dwell on it. The best thing was to carry on. Bishop Brown continued making his daily visits to the classroom. He would walk up and down the aisles, eyeing the students, not saying a word as the professor taught the lessons.

On the last day of the Bishop's stay, Tom was handed a note by his teacher that said the Bishop wanted to speak to him in his office at 2:00 P.M.

At one-fifty, Tom sat outside the Bishop's office, nervously watching the clock on the wall. When it struck two, he stood and tapped on the office door. A voice from inside instructed him to come in.

Bishop Brown sat in a high-backed chair behind a modest desk. His hands were folded neatly in front of him, and there was a thoughtful expression on his face. He looked to be in his mid-fifties, and he carried himself with an air of dignity.

"Please take a seat, son." He looked down at a sheet of paper in front of him. "Your name is Tom O'Neil?"

"Yes, sir."

"Where are you from, Tom?"

"I'm from a small farming town called O'Neil's Landing," Tom said.

"Tell me about your family."

"My father died when I was very young, so it's been me, my mother and two brothers for as long as I can remember. We were never wealthy and had to work hard year-round just to get by."

Bishop Brown nodded. "Tom, I have been reviewing your work and talking to the teachers about you. You're a very smart student, and know more about the Bible than anyone they have ever come across. Everyone agrees that you have what it takes to become a priest."

He leaned forward in his chair and laid his hands on the desk. "Tell me, Tom. Have you got what it takes?"

"If you're asking if I have the will and the faith, then yes, I do."

Bishop Brown stood up and stepped around his desk to offer his hand. "I know you'll succeed in what you came here to do. I wish you luck and May God bless you."

Tom left the Bishop's office that day feeling lighter than air. His nervousness vanished and he resumed his studies with a newfound purpose and determination. Each day he gave a silent prayer of thanks for his family, especially the father he never knew, but who had instilled in him early on, respect for the Word of God.

III

For what profit is it to a man if he gains the whole world, and lose his own soul? Or what will a man give in exchange for his soul?

Matthew 16:26

Be not overcome with evil, but overcome evil with good.

Romans 12:21

Chapter 17

MARY ANN DIDN'T KNOW the day to expect her son home from the seminary, just that it was sometime in July. She was tossing grain for the chickens one afternoon when a voice came from behind.

"Mother."

She spun around to see before her a tall young man dressed in black, and around his neck was a crisp white collar. At first she stared in shock, putting her hand to her mouth. Then she was in motion, and they were hugging.

"Tom," she sobbed. "Tom, you're a priest! Look at you!"

Seven years after Tom left O'Neil's Landing in search of his lot in life, he returned home to a hero's welcome. All of the Landing turned out to congratulate him. Among those who greeted him was Father Sheehan. Much had changed: William and David had married and stayed on the farm, and Johnny Connors had passed away.

The year Johnny died, Tom was sometimes despondent, and witnessing this, Bishop Brown arranged for his young protege to tutor on weekends and during the summer breaks. It was a welcome relief to Tom; it helped take his mind off his troubles and helped cover the tuition.

In the week of Tom's return, the O'Neils were visited by a continuous stream of well-wishers from town, including Mrs. Connors, whom he had visited every time he came home from college.

The locals rejoiced at Tom's return, and of course expected that he'd take over Father Sheehan's job. Word reached all corners of O'Neil's Landing that Tom O'Neil had returned. But not everyone was happy with the news.

Fred and Josephine McCourt didn't join in the festivities surrounding Tom O'Neil's success. They both knew without asking the other just how they felt about this turn of events. Fred's longstanding contempt for the O'Neils predated even his late wife's affinity for the O'Neil woman.

Fred poured a sherry and twirled the glass idly, thinking of the many deals he and his lawyer had sealed over the years, using bribery, extortion, and blackmail, all just means to an end.

Out of the corner of his eye Fred caught Jo biting a nail and staring into space.

"What?" he asked irritably.

Jo looked his way and lowered a hand from her face. "Oh," she said, flashing the sugar-sweet smile he hated so much, "nothing, Father."

He could tell something was on her mind, and he ventured he knew just what was bothering her. The O'Neil boy was back in town, and he had made quite a name for himself. Everyone in town was talking about him, and he knew it troubled his daughter to no end. He decided to have a little fun with it.

"What is it, Father?" It was Jo's turn to be annoyed when she heard her father let out a heavy sigh.

"Oh, nothing ... it's just that Widow O'Neil."

"What about her?"

"I don't know how she does it. First her husband dies and leaves her with three kids, and a farm to run. She has no money, yet she manages. I even tried to help her out one time by offering to buy her land." A shiver ran through him, remembering the day he thought Mary Ann was about to assault him with a garden spade.

He continued. "She's put one of her brats through the seminary, and look at him! A priest, of all things. A damn waste, if you ask me. She should have just given me the land when I asked for it."

He sipped his sherry and grinned against his glass when he noticed the scowl on his daughter's face. She didn't like to be reminded of others' successes in areas where she herself had failed. Her father knew she wasn't suited for teaching those many years ago, but at the time he didn't care. He just wanted to humiliate Tom and his whole sad family.

"We may have it yet," Jo said in a voice that made Fred shiver again.

The O'Neils were together once again, for the first time since Tom had gone to the seminary. The sun was setting behind the western mountains as they sat on their back porch that Monday evening. Tom was there, as well as Mary Ann, and David and William and their wives sat with them, enjoying the summer breeze.

Mary Ann spoke up as something occurred to her. "You know," she said, addressing David and William, "we're going to have to start calling your brother Father Tom from now on." Tom blushed, but his brothers roared with laughter. Their wives smiled at Tom good-naturedly.

"Father," Mary Ann said with a straight face, "you came home at the right time. Father Sheehan told us he is going to be transferred to another parish soon. Perhaps you should ask to take his place."

Tom grinned. "That's not a bad idea," he said. "I'll see if I can hold Mass this coming Sunday."

A month later, Tom received a letter from the Bishop saying that he was to stay in O'Neil's Landing and perform the duties of its parish priest. He was to move into the village and take up residence in the priest's house. He remembered the modest suite he had visited years ago to ask Father Sheehan to sponsor him into the seminary, and was pleased at the thought of being stationed in his hometown.

Tom spent the next few days moving into the parish house, with the help of his brothers. His mother accompanied them into town to help clean up his new home. Tom insisted that the parish priest had servants to help, but he relented when he saw the pained expression in his mother's eyes. In a week he was completely settled in.

Tom disliked being waited on by servants, but he grudgingly accepted the fact that his duties were too demanding for him to spend time on the chores he was once used to.

One evening, after a light supper, a knock came on the door and a servant entered. "Father," she said, "you have a visitor." Tom didn't look up from his book.

"Send them in, my dear."

He was reading when a voice made him look up. A beautiful young woman was standing in the doorway. He didn't recognize her at first, but there was something oddly familiar about her.

The woman stepped forward and said, "Hello, Father." Before he could respond she said, "You don't remember me."

"I'm afraid not."

"You don't remember one of your old classmates?"

"Oh, yes. Josephine McCourt."

"You do remember," she said, smiling.

Tom invited her to sit and called for tea.

They talked about their school days for a few minutes, when the servant knocked and entered a second time. She cast a hostile look at Jo before saying, "Father, if there's nothing more you need, I'll be going home for the night."

Tom smiled and waved a hand. "I'm fine, my dear. You can go."

She looked again at Tom's guest, and this time there was no mistaking it. She did not like Jo.

As soon as the door closed, Jo let out a laugh. "Father," she said with a smirk. "Why did you go to school for all those years? To waste it by becoming a priest?"

She laid down her empty cup. "What kind of life does a priest have anyway? Don't you see you've made a mistake, that you have gone astray? If you were to stay in the priesthood, your nights would be lonely and boring."

Tom couldn't believe what he was hearing. He was tempted to rush her out the door, but decided to let her have her say.

Jo's face had turned red. In a low voice she said, "Tom, I had planned for you to be my husband, and still do. Do you understand what I'm saying?"

"I understand what you're saying, and it cannot be," he said. "I have a calling, and will follow it till the day I die."

"We'll see about that," Jo said, and with that she stood. Flashing Tom a lascivious smile, she slowly began to undress herself.

"Stop that!" Tom shouted angrily. "Put your clothes back on and leave."

Jo's eyes never left his as she fixed her clothes and straightened her hair. She glared at him, then turned toward the door. After a moment's consideration, she spun around and said in a venomous tone, "Tom O'Neil, it would be in your best interest to reconsider. The McCourts have always had ways of getting what they want."

He said nothing, and when it became apparent he was not going to take her up on her offer, Jo stormed out of the office.

He collapsed in his chair, suddenly exhausted. It took him a few minutes to digest what had just happened. Tom had no idea Jo had ever felt so strongly toward him. Why would she make such a proposition now, when he was a man of the cloth?

Tom rose from his chair and gathered the cups and saucers. He would have cleaned them himself, but he suddenly felt tired. Leaving them for the servant, he retired for the night. He wasn't long asleep when he began to dream.

A large room. Many people were facing Tom but staring straight ahead. In front a man sat with his back to him, behind some huge ornate desk.

Suddenly the man turned around in his chair, and Tom was surprised to see it was his old friend, Johnny Connors. Tom was about to ask him what he was doing here, when the old man pointed a finger at him. At the signal, two burly men rushed forward and seized Tom.

Tom struggled, but the men were too strong for him. His hands and wrists were shackled behind his back. Everything went dark for a split-

second, and when he came to his senses he found himself in some dank, dark passageway. It was cold and wet, and Tom didn't need to explore his surroundings to know that there was no way out.

Tom awakened to a banging on the front door. Someone was calling. "Father! Father!"

Tom got out of bed and lit his oil lamp. He glanced at the clock, which said it was three o'clock in the morning. He ran down the hall to the door and found a scared-looking man standing in the porch wearing a nightshirt. Tom recognized him as one of his parishioners.

"It's my father. I think he may be dying."

Tom grabbed his coat and hat and rushed out the door, the disturbing dream soon forgotten.

Chapter 18

TWO WEEKS LATER, Tom's housekeeper suffered a heart attack and could work no more. He asked his mother to move in with him and take her place, reasoning that William and David had their own families and could take care of themselves. By moving in with him, he would get to see more of her.

Mary Ann was very happy to be taking care of one of her sons again, but it was to be short-lived. Three months after Jo had been at the parish's house, Tom and his mother were enjoying their noon meal when a knock came at the door. Tom opened it to see two uniformed men standing before him.

"Are you Tom O'Neil?" one of them asked.

"Yes."

"Was Miss Josephine McCourt here about three months ago?"

Tom looked from one man to the other. "Yes," he said slowly.

The second man pulled a badge from his coat pocket. "You're under arrest," he said. "Would you come with us, please?"

"There must be some mistake," Tom said.

"No mistake," the lawman said.

"What am I being charged with?"

"Rape."

Tom was stunned. "And who, may I ask, am I supposed to have raped?"

"Miss Josephine."

Tom O'Neil stood mutely in the doorway as the policeman slid the cold steel cuffs about his wrists. The words of his late friend Johnny Connors came back to him in haunting, prophetic clarity. *Stay away from that family.*

Mary Ann came to the door and trembled at the sight of Tom in handcuffs. She would have fallen to the floor had one of the officers not bent to support her.

"Mother," Tom said, "there is some mistake. This will be straightened out very soon."

The first officer cleared his throat. "You'll spend the night in jail here at O'Neil's Landing," he said matter-of-factly. "Tomorrow we'll start out for the city."

Tom tried to reassure his mother as he fell in step with the two officers for the short walk to the village jail. Tom was placed in a small cell, and one of the officers advised him, "I think you should get yourself a lawyer."

Tom stared at him. "I'm not guilty."

The lawman shrugged and walked away, leaving the young priest to his thoughts. The situation was grave. He had no witnesses to prove his innocence.

Three months earlier, Josephine McCourt had left the priest's house in a towering rage. Feeling more humiliated than she had ever thought possible, she hadn't trusted herself to return home that evening, but instead sought out one of the boarding houses she had frequented in her youth.

On her way, her fevered brain focussed on one thought: revenge. She would make that fool of a man pay dearly for refusing her. But how? Something had to be done, and done quickly. She ground her teeth in anger as the shame of being dismissed by that stupid O'Neil boy once again rose to the surface.

All night she paced the floor of the boarding house in frustration, revenge burning in her like a fiery ember. Her mind worked frantically to find a way to ruin Father Tom. At the very least, she would put him in his place.

The idea came to her so suddenly and with such perfect clarity, she wondered why she hadn't thought of it before. She bit her lip nervously. It was but a seed of a plan, but if it worked, not only would it put the O'Neil boy in his place, it would hurt him where it hurt most. Her teeth flashed in the darkness of her little room.

"Josephine," she murmured softly to herself, "get yourself out to the city as soon as possible." Still smiling, she lowered herself to her bed and fell into an untroubled sleep.

Early the next morning Jo hired a team and buggy for the trip outside town to her estate. She showed no mercy on the horses and cared little what the owner would think when they were returned to the livery stable. When she pulled into the estate yard, she barked an order to one of her father's hired hands to bring her own private team around to the front. "And see that the team I came in on gets back to town."

Fred McCourt was examing figures in a ledger when his daughter burst into his office. He looked up, a bemused smile on his lips. Jo's eyes had a slightly wild look to them, and he could tell there was something urgent weighing on her mind.

"I'm on my way to the city," she said simply.

Curiosity almost got the better of him, but Fred decided to keep his mouth shut. He knew better than to question his daughter about her comings and goings. She had an explosive temper that could flare up when least expected. In some ways she reminded him of himself.

Fred lowered his eyes once more to the ledger and pretended not to notice as his daughter scurried about his office. She removed a wad of bills from a wall safe, stuffed it into a travel bag, then reached in and snatched another. As an afterthought, she grabbed a bottle of whiskey from Fred's private stock and thrust it into the bag on top of the money.

In a minute, Jo was out the door and nodded to the hand who had brought her carriage around to the front yard. Fred watched in silence from his office window as the servant handed his daughter her whip after boarding her carriage. With a sharp command and a callous flick of her wrist, Jo prodded the stallions into a run.

Fred poured two fingers of scotch into a tumbler and stared at the vacant front yard. "I wonder," he said to the empty room, "what has got Jo in such a hurry this morning?" Not one to even care about the trouble his daughter was getting into, Fred perceived that there was something different about his daughter this morning. Did this have something to do with that priest, Tom O'Neil?

Fred had never liked Tom, or anyone else of the O'Neil clan for that matter. They had a way of making a person feel inferior just by looking at him. Frankly, he couldn't see what his daughter ever saw in him.

Everywhere, people were talking about the new priest and the good things he was doing at O'Neil's Landing. On every tongue in town were words of praise for Father Tom O'Neil, and the family.

They were amazed that Mary Ann had kept her family together all these years. Worst of all was the way the locals brimmed with respect for a family of dirt farmers.

Bile rose in Fred's throat as he remembered how his schoolmate, Tom O'Neil, had admonished him back when he was charged with rape. He felt no remorse for raping the young woman out in the field. His lawyer, Mr. Rourke, had siezed him a tidy plot of land in the process.

"That priest," Fred whispered, "is just like his father. Someday I'd like to see him get his."

Jo's team had neared the burnt-out campground that marked the halfway point between O'Neil's Landing and the railway station. Although reluctant to give her animals a rest, she couldn't have them collapsing in exhaustion before reaching the city.

Reining in the labouring horses, Jo saw that the old campsite was already occupied. A lone man sat beside a small fire. He either hadn't noticed her or paid her no heed. Tethered nearby, a roan horse grazed on what little grass there was to be had in this area. Jo guided her horses off the road to the riverside campground and climbed down from the carriage.

The smell of tea boiling over the fire reached Jo's nostrils. "Mind if I join you?" she asked the stranger.

"Happy to have you," the man said, still staring into the fire.

Jo walked toward the man and sat nearby. He looked up briefly and appeared startled that his fireside companion was a woman of beauty. She gave him an appraising look.

"Where are you headed?" she asked him.

"To the city."

"In a hurry to get there?"

"There's no one waiting for me, if that's what you mean," the man said, averting his eyes from hers nervously.

Perhaps I won't have to go all the way to the city after all, Jo thought. This man could help put her plan in motion. He would do nicely.

Jo was silent for a long time before she spoke again. When she did, she held the man's eyes with her own and spoke in tones that brooked no argument.

"I'll get right to the point. Would you like to earn yourself one thousand pounds?"

Her companion's mouth fell open. He turned to face her fully now, curious.

"There's a cabin that way about an hour's ride," Jo continued, gesturing to the south. "I want you to spend two nights with me."

The stranger swallowed hard. His eyes narrowed suspiciously. "One thousand pounds," he said slowly. "Did I hear right?"

"Yes, you heard right."

Jo could tell he knew a thing or two about women, and she knew what she was offering would be too tempting for such a man to resist. She was certain this fellow would go along just for the pleasure; money only sweetened the arrangement. Everyone had his price, the old McCourt credo stated.

As they drank tea and ate the sandwiches Jo had taken from home, her face split in a mischievous grin. "I want to be pregnant when we leave that cabin."

The stranger coughed and sputtered. "What?"

Jo laughed. "If you do what you're paid to do and keep your mouth shut," she said, her voice now deadly serious, "there's another thousand in it for you."

***

Two days later, Jo emerged from the cabin wherein she and the stranger had done the devil's work. She had waited inside while the man harnessed his horse and made ready to leave. She had asked him for a forwarding address, though she had no intention of paying the additional one thousand pounds. He had no idea who she was and that suited her fine. The man had done his job, she had paid him, and that was the last she ever wished to see or hear of him.

Hitching the team, she headed home. Her plan was ahead of schedule; there was no need to indulge in anonymous liaisons in the city.

Jo pulled into the yard of the McCourt estate late that evening. She bounded down off the carriage and handed the reins to her father's liveryman and went inside. Feeling hungry after the long day's ride, she flagged down the old woman who had served as the family's maid for as far back as Jo could remember. The old woman didn't like her much, but that hardly concerned Jo. As long as people did as they were told, they could keep their opinions.

Fred was in a foul mood when Jo came downstairs after bathing and changing into some clean clothes. Over the years, she had come to anticipate her father's mood swings, and she could tell what was on his mind this evening was no other than the O'Neil family. He was so deep in thought he neglected to ask her why she was home so early.

"What?" Fred snapped, looking up from some legal papers and noticing her for the first time.

"Oh, nothing, Father," Jo replied gaily, her eyes twinkling. "What's bothering you?"

Fred glared at her as she helped herself to some of his private stock. The decanter clinked softly back onto the silver tray as she laid it down. With a contented sigh she turned around and faced her father, sipping the cream sherry.

"Goddamn the O'Neil's," he said as if to himself, "and especially that young do-gooder of theirs. They're all anyone ever talks about these days."

Jo put down her glass. "Now, Father," she said consolingly, "don't get yourself worked up. You're likely to bring on a fit or a stroke." She folded her arms. "Besides," she added, "I don't think you'll have to worry about that family being in the town's good graces for too much longer."

Fred raised an eyebrow, but said nothing. He stared at his daughter for a long time, as if expecting her to say more, but instead she gave him a blank look and raised her glass to her lips again.

That evening, as darkness fell far to the east of O'Neil's Landing and the estate of the McCourts, a lone rider stopped to rest his horse. He dismounted and led the animal to a nearby stream. Crouching to refill his canteen with fresh running water, he winced as his stiff leg muscles protested. The man had ridden hard, perhaps as much to escape his guilty conscience as the woman who had helped put the guilt there.

These past two nights he had spent in the bed of a woman devoid of a soul. He was sure of this, as sure as he was that his own was now in question. He tried to blot out from his memory the last two days of his life, but he could not. Every hour, every minute he had spent with that nameless woman, stood out in stark accusation of him. Her motives for being with him were dubious, but he was no better a person for having accepted her offer.

"What have I done?" he asked his horse, who could only stare back at him and offer no answers. "I've committed a terrible sin, and now I can't help feeling someone is going to suffer for it."

Why had she wanted so badly for him to take her to bed? The urgency in her request troubled him. Surely any man would be only too willing to bed such an attractive woman, yet she had felt the need to offer him a fortune in pounds to seal what simply would have been an act of lust. Then there was the additional thousand she had promised.

That morning, he had noticed the word *Jo* painted on the side of the woman's carriage, and he wished he hadn't. It would have been far easier to live with his shame if the woman had remained nameless to him.

"But Jo, or whatever her name is, can keep her blood money," he confided to his horse. "I don't care to see her face again, or another shilling from her."

He rode hard that night through the dark countryside toward the sprawling city, away from his past and the name that would haunt him for the rest of his days.

Chapter 19

THE NIGHT BEFORE TOM was arrested, Jo went to her father's office and told him that his greatest wish was about to come true.

"How's that?" Fred asked.

"Rape," Jo replied.

Fred grunted. "When did this happen?"

"Three months ago tomorrow."

"And only now you let me know about it?"

"I had to make sure I had an open-and-shut case."

"And what makes your case so tight?"

"I'm pregnant. Is that proof enough?"

Fred slumped back in his chair. Pregnant! His only daughter was with child? He stared at her long and hard, suspicion creeping up on him that Jo was playing some kind of trick on him. But she only stood there, her face expressionless and her body language betraying nothing.

She broke the silence. "Tom O'Neil is the father." With that, she turned and walked out of his office.

Fred jumped to his feet, his mind working furiously on this bit of news his daughter had thrust upon him. There was an awful moment when the horrifying thought of being a grandfather to an O'Neil entered his mind. Rage rose like bile in his throat, at Tom O'Neil for intruding in his daughter's life—and, in turn, his own—and at Jo for allowing herself to become pregnant. He was not looking forward to having another child living under his roof, draining his coffers, and disturbing the quietude of his home that he had grown very fond of these past few years.

Fred paced the floor while the reality of his daughter's situation sank in. He was unhappy. Stopping only long enough to replenish his whiskey, he resumed pacing and tried to figure out a way to make this all go away. There was going to be a baby in the picture; he couldn't get around that. But as for the O'Neil boy ...

"Daughter! Get in here," he bellowed.

Jo looked a little too smug for Fred's liking when she swept into the room.

"You say Father Tom O'Neil raped you?" he growled.

"Yes," Jo replied. "At least, that's what the people of this town are going to believe." She gave him a mischievous wink.

Fred suddenly burst out laughing. The priest hadn't in fact raped his daughter, and in all likelihood never so much as laid a finger on her. This was too good to be true!

"There is the small matter of getting an attorney," Jo stated.

"I'll send for Rourke right away," Fred replied.

Jo smiled, and her father smiled back. She turned to leave, then stopped. "Oh, and Father," she said, looking over her shoulder at him.

"Yes?"

"Don't worry. I'm going to get rid of the baby."

Mary Ann rode as fast as she could for home. After the shock of seeing her son dragged away by two lawmen, she had locked the house and made haste to the livery stable in town to acquire a horse. The horse was closing the distance to the old farmstead at a swift gallop.

William came out of the barn at the same time David stepped out of the house, both curious at the sound of approaching hoofbeats. They were startled to see a panic-stricken Mary Ann wheel her horse into the front yard. Seeing William first, she darted toward her oldest son and flung herself off the horse. Tears ran down her cheeks, and her eyes had a slightly wild look to them.

"What's wrong?" he asked as he wiped his hands. David had walked over and now grasped his mother's arm to support her.

Mary Ann opened her mouth, but at first couldn't speak. The image of the two lawmen with Tom resurfaced and erased what she had planned to say to them. It took some time before she could say, "Tom has been arrested."

Mary Ann's daughters-in-law helped her into the house.

"What has he been arrested for?" William demanded. His face had gone pale with fright.

Mary Ann said simply, "Rape."

For the first time in his life, David swore in front of his mother. "That goddamn Jo."

William took his eyes off his mother's face and turned to his younger brother. "How do you know it's Jo?"

"William, isn't it obvious? I don't believe for a second that Tom committed any rape. But we know who's capable of laying such a charge on him, don't we?"

"But—"

"He's right, William," Mary Ann said, waving a hand at them to stop arguing. "Jo has pressed charges against your brother. The men who took him away said they will be bringing him to the city in the morning."

David stood up. "Then we'd better get over there."

The O'Neils walked into the jail and asked to see Tom. Mary Ann recognized the jailer as one of the men who had taken her son away. He nodded and said, "You can talk to him from outside his cell. You have five minutes."

When they turned the corner and saw Tom, they rushed over as one to talk to him. He was relieved to see them and took their hands in turn through the iron bars of his cell.

Mary Ann spoke. "I know you're not guilty, Tom, but I'm very worried."

Tom smiled. "Don't be," he said. "I'm not guilty, and this will all be straightened out in a day or two. I want all of you to stop worrying."

"I think we should get you a lawyer," William offered.

"No, I don't need one."

"Tom, you know the kind of people you're up against," Mary Ann warned.

She was about to say more, when the jailer approached them. Their five minutes were up, and Tom's family were asked to go. They were reluctant to leave him alone, but Tom reassured them.

"Everything will be all right, you'll see."

Her son's words were little comfort to Mary Ann, who had seen first-hand just how cruel the McCourts could be. She put up a brave front for his sake, but deep down she feared for her son's future.

Fred McCourt's carriage pulled up in front of the jail as the O'Neils were leaving. He suppressed a grin as he sidestepped them and continued up the steps and through the doorway. He was aware of their eyes following him, but he paid them no heed.

Inside, he proceeded to the nearest office. A guard seated at a desk looked up from the report he was perusing.

"Are you here to see the prisoner?"

"No," Fred stated as he closed the office door. "I'm here to see whoever is in charge."

"That would be me, sir."

"Good. I understand you're transferring Tom O'Neil to the city this morning?"

The jailer nodded. "That's the plan."

"Haven't you received word yet?" Fred asked. "Court will be held here in O'Neil's Landing, so don't waste your time." He reached into his coat pocket and withdrew a slip of paper.

The officer scanned the note and tucked it into his desk. "This isn't official. We'll wait until ten o'clock and if by then I don't have word, the prisoner will be transported."

A knock came on the door. The jailer excused himself and admitted a messenger with a telegram. It read, "Stay at O'Neil's Landing. Court will be held there on Tuesday of next week."

Fred smiled his first happy smile in a long time. Rourke, the lawyer, had come through. Fred had sent word to him late the previous evening, explaining the situation and what needed to be done, stressing that time was of the essence. *I want him tried and convicted right here, where everybody knows him,* the note to the lawyer had said.

When Fred left the police station that evening, he was humming, something he hadn't done in a long time.

Trials for serious charges such as those levelled at Father Tom O'Neil were a rarity in O'Neil's Landing. They were usually held in the imperious courthouses of the city. However, these were strange times, owing to Fred McCourt's influence on several key legal administrators. So, as had happened long ago when Fred himself stood accused of the very same crime, court would be held in this small town.

A large turnout was expected, so arrangements were made to secure a room adequate enough to hold the adjudication. After a quick survey, the courts found only one building able to hold the anticipated crowd. The irony was not lost on the townspeople, when it was decided that not only would their beloved priest be freed or condemned before their very eyes, but before the eyes of God Himself. The trial would be held in the church.

Tuesday morning dawned a steel grey over O'Neil's Landing. Outside the Roman Catholic church a large mob had amassed, eager to witness the momentous events unfold. Most were there to lend moral support to Tom O'Neil and his family, sure as they were of the family's impeccable character as they were that Miss Josephine McCourt was a villain of the worst order. Still, not a few of these men and women muttered unanswered questions outside the church that morning as to whether the charges laid against Father Tom were justifiable.

The great double doors at the front of the church admitted the waiting crowd. A scramble ensued to get seated, and those left standing were asked to leave.

Fred and Jo were the first to arrive. They made their way down the centre aisle and approached the massive oak altar which was to serve as the judge's bench. Neither met the gaze of any of the assembled crowd, and when they had reached the front of the church, they sat in their pews beside Stephen Rourke, the family's lawyer since time immemorial.

All were asked to rise, and the judge entered the courtroom from a side door. He sat behind the altar, and the bailiff motioned for the gathered crowd to take their seats as well. After consulting some notes, the judge looked up and nodded toward the back of the church. The guard opened a door, and two heavyset men entered. Between them, in leg irons, with his hands shackled behind his back, was Father Tom O'Neil. The crowd began to murmur when they saw him. He had dark circles beneath his eyes, but otherwise the priest appeared confident of the outcome of this trial. The judge silenced them with three sharp raps of his gavel on the altar, and the prisoner was led the rest of the way to his seat in silence.

When Tom was seated, another man stepped to the front of the courtroom and conferred with Jo and her lawyer before taking a seat beside them. He laid down his briefcase and from it withdrew some documents. These he handed to Mr. Rourke.

The judge cleared his throat. "Ladies and gentlemen, I am Judge William Claney. This court is now in session. Mr. Rourke," he continued, turning to Jo's lawyer, "you may proceed."

The old man who had served three generations of McCourts stood and turned side on to both Judge Claney and the gathered people from O'Neil's Landing. "Your Honour," he began, "Miss Josephine was raped three months ago and is now with child. I intend to prove to this court beyond a reasonable doubt that the accused, Tom O'Neil, is guilty of perpetrating this crime." He turned to the crowd and gave them a knowing look.

"Do we have any proof that Miss McCourt is pregnant?" Judge Claney asked.

The stranger at the McCourts' table stood and waved a document in the judge's direction. "Yes, we do, Your Honour," he said. "I'm a physician. I have examined Miss Josephine on two separate occasions and have concluded that she is with child."

The judge asked the bailiff to retrieve the document from the physician, then turned to Tom for the first time. "Mr. O'Neil, what do you have to say for yourself?"

Tom stood, the chain linking his leg irons rattling.

"How do you plead?" Judge Chaney asked.

"Not guilty."

"Very well. You may sit down."

Addressing Mr. Rourke, the judge said, "You may call your first witness."

"Your Honour. I have just one witness, the only one I'll need. I would like to call Miss Josephine McCourt to the stand."

The bailiff led Jo to the stand. He held out a Bible and asked her to put her hand upon it. "Do you swear to tell the truth, the whole truth, and nothing but the truth, so help you God?"

"I do."

As soon as the accuser sat, Mr. Rourke began pacing, his energy belying his age. "Miss Josephine, I know this is going to be hard on you, but I want you to tell the court what happened the night you visited Tom O'Neil." He paused. "What made you go to his house?"

Jo appeared to be trembling. "Well, Tom and I had gone to the same school. In fact, we were in the same class."

She looked up at her lawyer with a stricken look on her face. Rourke patted her hand and whispered to her some words of reassurance. He gave the crowd a sober look to elicit sympathy for his client.

"He was a bright student," Jo continued in a soft voice. "He did well in school. We didn't see each other very often after we finished our education; he had been away at the seminary a year or more before I'd even heard about it.

"When he came back, I wanted to go over to the O'Neils' house to congratulate him, but I decided to wait. There were so many people going over there when he came back, and I wanted to talk to him alone to catch up on old times. Before long, he had moved into the parish house in town. I visited him shortly after that.

She stopped and dabbed her eyes with a handkerchief. The judge asked her if she would like the court to take a short recess, but she refused the offer.

Rourke continued his questioning. "Who was there at the house when you arrived?"

"Tom and the housekeeper."

"Please go on, Miss McCourt."

Jo put away her handkerchief and leaned forward, her voice stronger this time.

"Tom told the housekeeper to go home. Of course, I didn't think anything of it at the time. When she left, he poured himself a drink and offered me one. I took it and we talked for a little while. I finished my drink and got up to leave, and he offered me another. I told him it was getting late and that I had to leave, but he poured another one for me anyway.

"I insisted that I really had to go. When he saw that I wasn't going to take the drink from his hand, he got angry. He smacked the glass down on his desk and grew red in the face. 'I'll be honest with you,' he told me. 'All those years away I have found myself thinking about you more and more. I want you and mean to have you.'

"I was frightened. I knew that look in his eyes. He made a grab at me but I backed away. I turned to leave, but I was so scared I stumbled and fell to the floor. Then he was there and he had his hands on the buttons of my dress. He was like a madman! I couldn't believe what was happening. I was so shocked I couldn't move."

Tears were streaming down Jo's face as she continued. "He ... he c-carried me to his bedroom and threw me on the bed. He tore off my clothes and f-forced himself on me. There was nothing I could do! I screamed for help but there was no one else in the house. He hurt me ...

"And when he was done, he ... he told me to get dressed and to get out of his house. He looked very angry when he said I had better keep my mouth shut. I truly believe he intended to kill me if I said anything about it."

Mr. Rourke said in a voice that was almost a whisper, "Thank you, Miss McCourt. I have nothing further, Your Honour."

Judge Claney put a finger to his lips and sat in silence for a moment. A slow murmur began to spread amongst the townspeople in the courtroom, and this he silenced with his gavel.

"Mr. O'Neil, are you representing yourself?"

Tom stood. "Yes, Your Honour, I am."

"Do you have anything you want to ask Miss McCourt?"

"No, Your Honour."

"Very well. You may step down, Miss McCourt. Please help her to her seat, Mr. Rourke."

The old lawyer helped a sobbing Jo to her feet and led her back to their table.

Mary Ann watched the drama unfolding before her with gritted teeth. It took everything she had within her not to scream in outrage. She never once doubted her son was innocent of the charge laid against him, but to see that girl put on this show of deception made her tremble with rage.

Many years ago, Mary Ann had thrown a birthday party for Tom at their house. Jo hadn't been invited, but she had shown up anyway. She could only watch in frustration as Jo had circulated amongst Tom's classmates, spreading rumours about this one and that one. The girl had always been a gifted actress, to be sure, but where once only a child's reputation was on the line, now her son's very life was at stake.

Then there was Jo's lawyer, this Mr. Rourke. This was a man who was capable of tipping the scales when a person's life hung in the balance. He had utterly ruined one family many years ago, back in the time when Fred McCourt had been a young man. A young girl who had had the misfortune of being in the wrong place at the wrong time found herself on the receiving end of a lawsuit. She had to defend her honour when it was certain that she had been the one who had suffered at Fred's lascivious hand.

This lawyer, the same one who had turned a victimized young girl into a bloodthirsty criminal in the eyes of the court, was now about to ruin another life. How could one man have so much power? Until now, Mary Ann didn't know it was possible to feel so small and helpless, like a pawn on a chessboard. Although she was ashamed to admit it, as he was little more than a pawn himself to the cruel whims of the McCourts, she hated him all the same.

"If you're ready, Mr. O'Neil, you may proceed."

Mary Ann watched with her heart in her throat as her son shuffled to the witness stand, laid his hand on the Bible and swore to tell the truth, the whole truth, and nothing but the truth, and took his seat.

"What I have to say won't take long," he began, "and what I have to say will be the truth. I have no witnesses, Your Honour, but I must say this. I don't know if Jo wilfully lied, or if she remembers that night differently than I do, but what she told the court this morning did not happen."

Mr. Rourke shot to his feet. "Objection! Your Honour, it is for this court to decide if my client's testimony is the truth, *not* Mr. O'Neil."

He seemed to want to say more, but the judge waved a hand at him to sit down. "Please continue, Father O'Neil."

Tom shook his head. "I did not force her to drink anything. I asked her if she would like something to drink, and she asked for wine. I did not tell the housekeeper to leave—she left on her own. But more importantly, I did not touch that woman.

"Your Honour, there are three in this courtroom today who know the truth."

The judge raised his eyebrows. "Oh? Who might they be?"

"They are Tom O'Neil, Josephine McCourt, and God," Tom said as he stood. He turned and looked at his mother. "The third one I named, the One who knows all things, will set me free."

This set off another round of murmuring among the crowd.

"Order! Order in the court," Judge Claney barked, smacking his gavel down hard on his desk.

Tom stood and shuffled back to his table.

The judge asked both Tom and Mr. Rourke, "Gentlemen, is there anything else?"

Tom shook his head, but Mr. Rourke got to his feet. "Your Honour," he said, then turned to face the people from O'Neil's Landing, "it has been proven to this court beyond a shadow of a doubt that Tom O'Neil had carnal knowledge of my client without her consent.

"Miss Josephine McCourt, an upstanding citizen of O'Neil's Landing, through no fault of her own must now live her life in shame. This man, this priest," he said, gesturing at Tom, "has fooled the good people of O'Neil's Landing. He is in fact a man of low character whose behaviour is beneath any man in a position of trust such as his. But the worst tragedy of all is this act of violence has created a child in this woman. Mr. O'Neil has victimized not only one person. He has ruined two lives."

Mary Ann watched the faces in the crowd, and her heart sank. They were breathless. Mr. Rourke had given a voice to what was in their hearts, but which they couldn't articulate. Their priest had betrayed them. Their spiritual leader, their moral compass, was a fraud. He had made fools of them, and now after Mr. Rourke's speech, a look of despair was reflected on every face, a look of dismay, disillusionment, and defeat. Mary Ann felt a cold certainty clutch her heart.

Nodding when he saw that his words had hit home, Jo's lawyer said to the judge, "I am asking the court for a sentence of not less than twenty years of hard labour. The only verdict in this case is *guilty*."

Judge Claney adjourned the court and retired to the side room. Jo, her father, and Mr. Rourke leaned together, deep in discussion, while Tom sat pensively at his table. Mary Ann tried to get his attention, and when he looked her way she didn't see in his eyes what she knew in her heart was about to happen. Looking beyond today held little promise for Mary Ann.

For the next ten minutes the crowd muttered angrily amongst themselves. Then the judge returned, and a hush as still and silent as death fell over the courtroom.

Judge Claney clasped his hands together in front of him, the expression on his face unreadable. He looked at Josephine

McCourt, the plaintiff, then at Tom O'Neil, the defendant. He spoke.

"I have carefully reviewed the testimony given in this court today. Tom O'Neil, I find you guilty as charged. Do you have anything to say for yourself before I pass sentencing?"

"Yes, I do, Your Honour."

Tom stood and with tears in his eyes faced the people seated in the church. Most of them he had known all his life, but not until he had taken over the town's pastoral duties had he come to know all of them on a personal level. He considered them a second family.

"This court has just convicted an innocent man. But I have faith. I believe God will shed a new light on me before this is all over, and that someday, in your eyes, I'll be the man you always knew me to be. This is a sad day, but there'll be a better one for us all.

"I am only a man, one who has been judged and found guilty by other men, but the Heavenly Father knows all. He will see justice done. I ask you to keep Him in your hearts; do not turn Him away."

Mary Ann sobbed in her seat as William and David steadied her. She couldn't bear to raise her eyes to see her son face his judgment, but each word the judge said rang clear in her mind and would haunt her to the end of her days.

"Father Tom O'Neil, I sentence you to fifteen years of hard labour. Take the prisoner away."

The sound of his gavel banging on his desk came to Mary Ann like the slamming of a massive door, its note of finality reverberating in her memory long after it ceased.

And so it was that Tom O'Neil—beloved priest, son, and now convicted criminal—was led from the church in shackles to serve a long sentence for a crime he didn't commit. The community of O'Neil's Landing was saddened at the loss of such a man who had been dear to their hearts, for even though he had been found guilty under Irish law, God's law was irrefutable, and many a man, woman, and child's faith in that town could not be swayed or shaken by this mockery of justice.

O'Neil's Landing, and indeed all of Ireland, would not soon forget the downfall of one of its greatest spiritual leaders. Throughout the country, the newspapers of the day carried the story of how a once great man had betrayed the people he had served. Fred McCourt made sure of that.

Chapter 20

IN TIME, THE TRIAL against a young priest in a small Armagh town grew unimportant and was all but forgotten.

Life had never been better for the McCourt clan. Fred travelled the country several times over in the seven years since the trial. His business enterprises grew ever more prosperous. He pulled strings here and there, implemented hostile takeovers whenever small upstart companies began to pose risks to his monopolies, and threatened the appropriate officials whenever necessary. His political clout was far-reaching.

During those first few years after Tom O'Neil had been found guilty, McCourt had kept his ear to the ground and listened—with an almost perpetual half-smile—to the local gossip. Wherever his travels took him, people were outraged at the scandal surrounding the Catholic priest. Religion was a big deal in this country, and the general consensus was that the priest had not only turned his back on the people in his hometown, but had given a bad name to Roman Catholics everywhere. Life was good. Fred was wealthier than he had ever dreamed possible, his enemies were as dust, and his daughter only showed her face whenever she needed money. He didn't mind; in fact, he felt a certain grudging respect for the girl. She had, after all, been the one to deliver the *coup de grâce* to the biggest thorn in his side.

After Tom had gone to jail to begin his long sentence, Jo went to the city. Fred had made arrangements for her to meet with a midwife and stay with her in a boarding house until the time came when she would give birth. The midwife was instructed to take the baby away once it was delivered. Fred didn't care what happened to it, as long as it disappeared. Whenever anyone asked about Jo's baby, he and his daughter had donned a mournful expression and said that it had died at birth.

Jo had never been cut out for motherhood. She felt no remorse for the loss of her baby. She had never wanted the child in the first place; it was just a means to an end. After ridding herself of it, she stayed in the city and lived in luxury, in a small estate her father had procured especially for her. Life was good for her as well, and sometimes she would think back on the town whose illusions she had shattered, and the priest whose spirit she had crushed and whose body was condemned to a lifetime of hard labour—and she would smile.

Lately, though, Jo had grown tired of the city's social life. The lavish parties she threw at her manor were beginning to tire the flighty debutante, and she felt she needed some change of scenery. Each day that passed here in the bustling city, each carriage ride through the city proper, each expensive gift and proposal for marriage she received from some over-eager would-be suitor, irritated her more and more. Restless, she sent word to her father that she would like to spend some time with him back home.

He sent word back to her that he would arrange for Mr. Rourke to act as agent in the sale of her city estate, and he would meet her at the railway station when she decided to make the move.

Peter Cash lived his life these days as a travelling salesman for farm machinery. He had worn many hats in his day, as was common for many of Ireland's young men in search of an honest dollar. This job was by far the greatest in which he had ever taken part. His travels took him near and far, he got to taste the freedom of the open road, and he enjoyed meeting new people. He was good at it, too. Mr. Patrick Murphy always provided him with a generous expense allowance in return for what he knew would be a huge new client list from his best field agent.

He had just checked in with Mr. Murphy and handed over a list of farmers' addresses for his boss to follow up on. The two of them wore identical grins as they sat and downed a celebratory drink and smoked a few of the employer's finest cigars. There was still much more to be done. Armagh and surrounding counties were areas still largely untapped. Peter's next assignment was to secure clients there in need of farm machinery. He was to leave in the morning, so Mr. Murphy wished a safe journey and advised him to get a good night's sleep.

In the morning, Peter made his way to the train station, bought his ticket, and handed his baggage to the attendant. He boarded and went immediately to the dining car. Feeling he deserved a hearty breakfast after his most recent success in sales, he sat and ordered a generous platter of eggs, sausage, toast, and a mug of tea.

He was partway through breakfast when the train began to move. This had always been his favourite part of train rides, watching as familiar buildings and hills and forests and ponds whisked by and made way for the new scenery. Peter looked out the window with a wistful expression on his face before turning his attention back to his half-finished meal.

New arrivals started pouring into the dining car as Peter leaned back with a full belly. He sipped his third cup of tea and watched the strangers file in. Laying down his tea and checking his pocket watch, he was about to stand and find his car, when he froze. A woman had just entered the dining car and looked his way. Recognition had not dawned on her face, but he thought he knew her from somewhere. In fact, he was certain of it.

Slowly, he walked the length of the dining car and into the adjoining cars to find his seat. The conductor soon came by on his rounds, and as he passed, Peter pulled him aside to ask a question.

"I just saw a lady in the dining car a couple of minutes ago. She was about thirty, with long dark hair. Very pretty. Do you know who she is?"

"Why do you ask, sir?"

"Oh, I think she is someone I used to know. Where is she from?"

The conductor looked in the general direction of the dining car. "I believe she is from O'Neil's Landing," he said after a moment's thought.

"Do you know her name?"

"She goes by the name Miss Josephine."

Peter shook his hand. "Thank you. I was mistaken."

The conductor smiled. "Don't worry, I get that a lot."

O'Neil's Landing ... why does that name ring a bell? Peter thought. He had heard the name before, but he couldn't place it. He had never been there before, he knew that much, but for some reason the name tickled his memory. The woman in the dining car, though, he was almost sure he had crossed paths with her in the past. He hadn't had a sound night's sleep as Murphy had advised, and tiredness, combined with the heavy breakfast, made him doze.

When Peter woke, he looked out the window at unfamiliar grasslands. He watched as they rolled by, not thinking about anything in particular, until the woman he had seen in the dining car crept back into his thoughts. *Miss Josephine.* Curiosity got the better of him, so he stood and found himself walking once more in the direction of the dining car.

Peter drew in a sharp breath when he entered. Miss Josephine was staring directly at him. But again, she didn't seem to recognize him. He looked away and hoped she didn't detect any of his uneasiness. Trying to act casual, Peter strolled along the aisle past her table.

Suddenly, the woman's hand shot out and touched his wrist. Peter's blood ran cold.

"Stranger, do you have the time?" Miss Josephine asked him.

Peter swallowed, desperately hoping his voice wouldn't crack when he spoke. Without looking at her, he said, "Yes, ma'am. It is now eleven-fifteen."

His heart throbbed painfully in his chest as he hurried down the aisle and took a seat at one of the dining tables. He watched the woman's back from his vantage point, and he determined that he would stay out of her sight for the remainder of the trip.

The train stopped at midafternoon. Peter had so far managed to avoid Miss Josephine by staying in his seat. Having grown tired of sitting for so long, he decided he would risk getting up and stretching his legs. He entered an adjoining car and almost collided with Miss Josephine. This was her stop. Peter decided to step off and have one last look at the woman who troubled him.

Stepping outside into the cool afternoon air, Peter looked down the length of the train and saw the woman boarding a fancy carriage hitched to a pair of black stallions. Feeling brave, Peter walked along the rail cars and approached the woman's carriage. Along the sideboards was written one word: JO.

It was suddenly clear. He'd seen that carriage before. He knew the woman better than any unmarried man had any business to. Miss Josephine was the woman who had paid him a thousand pounds to make her pregnant.

But where is the child? This question plagued Peter Cash for the rest of the day as he sat brooding in his seat. Had the woman's plan worked? Had she become pregnant during the two nights she and Peter had spent in the roadside cabin seven years earlier? Perhaps not.

He never did spend the money she had given him. For several years after his encounter with the woman, he had kept the pounds safely tucked away, never giving it a second thought, even when his own money was scarce and he was forced to spend nights sleeping under the stars. It was blood money, he was sure of that. Somewhere, someone was suffering from the pact he had made with this terrible woman.

Peter had often thought about the possibility he had fathered a child. Was it a boy? A girl? He regretted spending those nights in the cabin with that woman. For weeks on end he would awake from nightmares about a child he didn't know.

These thoughts were driving him crazy. He had to keep himself occupied, had to keep moving, and so he had sought employment in his current trade. Mr. Murphy was a fair boss who kept him on the road, and in time, Peter forgot about his roadside affair.

He knew now where he had heard the name O'Neil's Landing. A few years back, there wasn't a soul in Ireland who hadn't read about the priest who had raped some local woman. Peter was not overly religious, but he remembered feeling a sense of moral outrage at the time.

O'Neil's Landing was becoming a very curious place.

That evening, Peter disembarked in a town called Hammerdown. It was a small place, but possessed all the amenities a travelling salesman needed: a hotel, a restaurant, and a pub. This was not a scheduled stop, but Peter made good use of his time. He circulated among the locals and managed to garner some interest in Mr. Murphy's farm machinery. On the third day in town, satisfied that he had exhausted all avenues of possible sales, he decided to relax.

That evening, Peter ordered a large meal at the restaurant and then went to the pub. Few people frequented the drinking establishment, he found, as he stepped through the doors. A scattered couple sat here and there deep into their cups, and several loners leaned a little too far in their seats. Peter stepped up to the bar and ordered a whiskey.

The bartender smiled at Peter, and he knew right away that this was the place where he would get the information he needed.

"My good man, how far is it to O'Neil's Landing?"

"An hour or two," the barkeep replied. "Do you intend to go there?"

"Maybe," Peter said. "I'll have another whiskey, and pour one for yourself, too."

"Thank you, sir."

"Isn't that the town I read about in the paper a couple of years back? Didn't someone rape a woman there?"

The bartender's eyes lit up. Soon he was regaling Peter with stories of the O'Neils and the McCourts and the trial that shook O'Neil's Landing. It was a small, peaceful village, he told Peter, and the scandal was too much for the people there to handle. They had lost faith in man and God alike, and now the place was only a shadow of its former self.

The barkeep leaned in close. "But I believe Father Tom was railroaded from the very beginning. And I'm not the only one."

"How's that?" Peter asked.

"Well, the woman he was supposed to have raped is not to be trusted. She and her father were always up to no good; ask anyone, and they'll tell you. It wouldn't be the first time Fred McCourt used his wealth to get what he wanted, and he'd always had it in for the O'Neils. There's some kind of family feud there that goes back a couple of generations.

"That girl had the best lawyer her father's money could buy. I'm not the only one who will tell you this—he paid off the judge and the doctor."

"What doctor?"

"The McCourts had a doctor on their side."

"What for?" Peter asked

"To prove that she was pregnant."

A sudden chill ran up Peter's spine. "And tell me, sir, what was the girl's name?"

"Oh, that's Josephine McCourt. But everyone in town calls her Jo. I think she moved up to the city some years back."

Peter's hands were shaking. An innocent man had been imprisoned, a priest, no less. He was horrified to think how low a person could be to set into motion the lies, the manipulation, and the legal proceedings necessary to carry out such an injustice. And he himself had been an unwitting participant in the priest's wrongful imprisonment. *That's what she needed me for! What have I done?*

"I can't believe it," he said in an awed voice.

"What was that?" the bartender asked.

"Oh, nothing," Peter said quickly. "Is the priest's family still living around there?"

"Yes. They still live at O'Neil's Landing."

Peter thanked the man and paid for the drinks. In the street, his thoughts reeled. He had to do something. The sins he had committed had caused a man of the cloth to be convicted of a crime that never happened!

All night he lay awake in his hotel room. The only thing for him to do at this point was to talk to the priest's family. He would tell them of his encounter with Josephine McCourt. He shuddered. This was a woman who would stop at nothing to get her way. He didn't know what this girl could possibly have against Father Tom O'Neil, but he intended to find out.

The next day, Peter travelled to O'Neil's Landing.

Chapter 21

FRED MCCOURT SAT BEHIND his desk in his estate's study, nursing a glass of whiskey, reminiscing. He and Jo had arrived the previous day after attending business in town. Jo hadn't complained too much about the delay and being around her brought back a lot of memories.

"How long has it been?" he said. "Six, seven years? It only seems like yesterday that O'Neil brat was sweating out his last few minutes as a free man." He laughed.

It struck him how alike he and his daughter were. They both had the right stuff to succeed in life. To survive in this world you had to be brave enough to take what you wanted, and you couldn't afford to be squeamish over how you got it. Jo's mother didn't have what it took, and so she had taken the coward's way out. It made no difference to Fred, though. The world was built for the strong; there was no room for weaklings.

Sheilagh had taken a liking to that O'Neil woman, too, and it had never sat right with Fred. They were do-gooders, but poor. This caused a flicker of annoyance to cross Fred's face. Since

Father Tom had gone to jail he had twice made the Widow O'Neil generous offers to buy her land. Twice she refused.

McCourt leafed through some papers on his desk until he found what he wanted. Perhaps this time she wouldn't be so quick to refuse his offer.

Fred had learned that the O'Neils were attempting to get a retrial for the priest. Rourke was his ace in the hole; he was confident that the lawyer could punch holes in whatever paltry new evidence the O'Neils thought they had. And if that failed, he could always call in a favour from certain judges. Were the O'Neils desperate enough to see their boy go free that they would sell their farm? He counted on it.

But there was one thing that bothered him. Father Tom O'Neil hadn't gotten Jo pregnant; he was completely innocent. Who had, then? He had pried her for an answer once, and her only response was, "You don't have to worry about that. I don't know him, and he wouldn't know me if he passed me on the street."

Fred wasn't satisfied. This was a loose end, one that couldn't be taken care of now.

Peter Cash rented a rig, intending to start out early in the morning for the O'Neil farm. At the livery stable, he struck up a conversation with the owner.

"I'm headed for O'Neil's Landing. I heard there was some kind of trouble up that way a couple of years back."

The old man blinked. "You must not be from around here, then. Well, a priest by the name of Tom O'Neil got himself into a bit of trouble with one of the local girls. She said he raped her, he said he didn't, and the law sided with her ..." His voice trailed off.

"What else?" Peter asked.

"Sir, I don't know the truth of it any more than you do, but I think the law was wrong to convict Father Tom. Those McCourts are a rotten bunch. Just ask anyone who's ever had dealings with them."

"What kind of people are the O'Neils?" Peter asked.

The livery owner looked him straight in the eye. "You'll not find better people in your travels."

Peter took possession of the horse and rig and set out for O'Neil's Landing. He didn't stop for breakfast. He felt every idle minute weighing heavily on his soul. Pushing the horses, he chased the road with renewed vigour, pausing only long enough to cast a wary glance at the campground where he had collided with fate seven years earlier.

In the seven years that Tom was in prison, a sombre atmosphere had settled into the O'Neil household. Mary Ann and her sons spoke in hushed tones, their spirit having left them so long ago, that now it seemed a dream. William and David continued their daily chores without a contrary word. They looked hardship in the face and did what had to be done. This had always been the O'Neil way.

The family had recently stirred from their former sadness. David's wife had suggested to Mary Ann one day that they try and raise enough money to get Tom's case reopened. This sparked a little hope in her, and for months she had worked longer and harder hours at cultivating the gardens that dotted their farm. The boys watched her with a dull ache in their chests. Both of them knew that, even if they could re-examine their brother's case, they could bring forth no new evidence, and the verdict would inevitably be the same as before.

They remained silent, however, and let their mother have her way. It had given her a new sense of purpose so they held their tongues.

The family was sitting at breakfast discussing the sutuation.

"I spoke to a lawyer today," Mary Ann said without looking up from her plate. "We're still three hundred pounds short."

William and David shared an uneasy look. This was only half of the lawyer's asking price.

"That's a lot of money," David said feebly.

Mary Ann nodded. "I think the man is being honest with us. He told me the prosecution has a pretty strong case. 'Cut and dry' is how he put it. He also said it would be pointless to re-examine the case anyway unless we have new evidence."

"Mother," William said in a soft voice, "David and I have talked this over. If you think it will help to reassess Tom's case, then we will help you do it. I don't know, maybe the judge will change his mind. But we can't sit by and watch you work yourself to death."

"What are you saying?"

"We'll sell the farm," David said.

Mary Ann was shaking her head before the words left David's mouth. "Tom wouldn't hear of it. The last time I visited him I suggested the same thing. He said the place rightfully belongs to you and William."

"How can he talk like that?" David asked. "I say we sell it."

Mary Ann held up a hand. "We will not be selling our land. Do you remember when Fred tried to buy us out?"

David and William nodded.

"This is just what he wants. If we give in and sell our farm, he will have taken everything from us. Everything. I can't throw away all the years your father and grandfather put into making a home the O'Neils could call their own."

William was about to say something, but he was interrupted by a knock on the door.

"I won't hear any more of this talk," Mary Ann said as she got up and went to the door. She straightened her clothes and opened it to see a young man of about thirty years of age.

"Are you Mrs. O'Neil?" he asked.

"Yes, I am."

"My name is Peter Cash," the young man said. "I'm a travelling salesman for farming equipment, but that's not what I'm here for."

The young man cast his eyes downward. "I ... I have some information you may be interested in. May I come in?"

Mary Ann suddenly remembering her manners. "Oh, please do. Come into the kitchen. We are having breakfast. Are you hungry?"

"You're very kind, ma'am."

Mary Ann set another place and introduced Peter to the family. "Mr. Cash says he has some information he wishes to share with us. Sir, we don't keep secrets from each other, so you can tell us after you have eaten."

He thanked Mary Ann and dug into a plateful of ham and eggs. Mary Ann next placed a platter of toast and a dish of homemade butter in front of him. The dusty ride out had made him raveneous. When he had his fill, Peter pushed his plate away and got down to business.

"Mrs. O'Neil, I don't know how to tell you this. This is very difficult for me; I've never had to say such things to a woman before. But I have to tell you, and you have to listen."

Mary Ann gave her sons a worried look. Then she turned back to the young man sitting at her table.

"Do you have a son who is a priest?" Peter asked.

"Yes."

"Is he in prison?"

"He is."

"All right," Peter said. "You may not like what I have to tell you. I unknowingly put your son in prison."

Mary Ann gasped. William and David and their wives looked at Peter with shock on their faces.

Slowly, Mary Ann said, "But, Mr. Cash, you couldn't have had anything to do with it. You weren't even there."

William was angry. "Explain yourself!"

Peter had expected this reaction. "What you say is true, but I did play some small part in it."

"What are you trying to tell us?" David demanded.

"Mrs. O'Neil, tell me. The woman your son supposedly raped ... was she pregnant?"

"Yes. She said in her statement that she was three months along."

"I'm certain," Peter said, "that I'm the father of that child." He looked around the table and saw identical expressions of confusion, so he continued. "Three months before the charges, I was at an old campground to the east. I remember it like yesterday, even though I've been trying to forget it all this time. A woman came along and shared a drink with me. She had one of the finest teams I've ever seen." He broke off, suddenly embarrassed.

Mary Ann patted his hand. "It's all right, Mr. Cash. You can tell us. Take your time."

Peter smiled. He cleared his throat and continued. "She asked me if I wanted to earn some money. I didn't know what she had in mind, so I asked her what I would have to do. Well," Peter said, blushing, "she said she wanted me to take her to bed. Not only that, she wanted to make sure I got her pregnant. She promised me even more money afterwards if I kept my mouth shut."

A mystery that had haunted the O'Neil family for seven years was finally beginning to unravel. Over these years, neither O'Neil doubted Tom's innocence, but proving he hadn't raped Josephine McCourt was a different matter entirely. Mary Ann poured Peter some more tea and thanked him for the information.

"I've always regretted what I had done, Mrs. O'Neil. Somehow I guess I always knew someone was being made to suffer for my sins. This woman was offering me money, but why? I'm sure she would have had no trouble finding herself a man.

"I saw her on the train a couple of days ago. She didn't see me, but I thought I knew her from somewhere. So I asked around to find out who she was and where she was from. Sure enough, she was the same woman who had accused your son of rape, and the same one who had paid me to get her pregnant."

"May I call you Peter?" Mary Ann asked.

"Yes, of course."

"Peter, if we can raise enough money to get Tom's file reviewed, will you tell the authorities what you told us today?"

"I would gladly do so."

William spoke up. "Peter, I wouldn't make it public what you have just told us. Fred and Jo are very powerful people. I don't think there's anything they wouldn't do to keep you from talking."

Peter appeared to be deep in thought. "Mrs. O'Neil," he said then, "you say you're trying to raise enough money for a retrial?"

Mary Ann nodded.

"Well," he said, "I still have the money Miss Josephine gave me."

Chapter 22

IT WAS ALWAYS COLD in here. Cold and damp. It felt like a tomb, and the similarities between the two didn't escape Father Tom O'Neil. For one thing, his cell block was underground. For another, everyone in here was either dead or dying. He had seen countless bodies carried out, to be buried without even a casket. The place smelled of rot and of human waste.

Not surprisingly, Tom and his fellow inmates welcomed the coming day and the hard labour that awaited them. They felt blessed to escape their frigid quarters, if only for a short time. The work was hard, brutal. Sore muscles, aching backs and rheumatic fingers were commonplace for the prisoners of St. William's Jail, but each man agreed that they would prefer pain and discomfort to the fevers that carried so many of their fellows away.

Breakfast was a grisly affair. The gruel that served as their meals made the food Tom had eaten at the monastery look like a gourmet feast. When he had first arrived at the prison, Tom weighed two hundred pounds. Now, he guessed he weighed about one hundred and fifty.

He missed his family very much. Memories of his days on the farm, working with his brothers, sitting down to his mother's home-cooked meals, and the days when his best friend Johnny Connors was alive flooded back to him on days when his loneliness was keenest. He dreamed of horseriding and fishing expeditions and the trek he had taken into the mountains to Johnny's cabin. It was there he had made the decision to become a man of the cloth.

He prayed. Every day and night in his small, dank cell Tom prayed and sought God's guidance. God had not abandoned him. It was man's actions that had shoved him in harm's way. God was infallible, but man was not. This was the cross he had to bear. God's will was not for him to know, and he would not question or doubt Him. Tom's faith was still strong, and it carried him as it always had from one day to the next, and he believed that a new day would arrive and bring with it better news than the last.

And he dreamed. Some nights when he was not sure if he was sleeping or awake, Fred and Jo McCourt entered his dreams. It was always the same. Jo would call his name as if from far away, and pointing at him, would say to her father, *We always get what we want, don't we, Daddy?* The two of them would laugh and turn away. The most curious part of this recurring dream, though, was the mysterious third person who always stayed just a step or two behind the McCourts. He was a young man about Tom's age, but he didn't know who he was. The stranger never smiled, but only stared at him, mouthing words Tom couldn't understand.

One morning, after prayers, a guard came to his cell and announced that he had a visitor and a bath would be arranged.

"You're a lucky man, O'Neil. Not everyone in here gets to bathe more than once a month."

It was customary for guards to announce visitors a day in advance. This would give them time to clean the prisoner, cut his hair, and make him presentable to the outside world. The warden hid the truth of his prisoners' living conditions from outsiders, and those who gave thought to exposing how horrible life was on the inside were threatened with severe beatings and starvation. Tom had seen it happen more than once, and more often than not a prisoner succumbed to his punishment and was silenced forever.

Tom sat on the board that served as his bunk. He couldn't imagine who could be coming; his mother had seen him not two weeks ago. But he could give it no more thought for now, as the sound of a nightstick banging on his bars signalled the beginning of the prisoners' workday.

The next day Tom was awakened to a guard entering his cell carrying a coarse cloth and a bowl filled with hot water. Another came in carrying a razor. When they were satisfied he was clean enough, he was shackled and led out of his cell to a separate building.

He was surprised to see his mother.

"Tom, I had to see you again! There is someone I want you to meet."

She turned and called out to a man standing not far away. He walked toward them, and when Tom saw his face for the first time, he drew in a sharp breath.

"You! You're the man from my dreams."

"What are you talking about?" Mary Ann asked, startled.

"This fellow: I've seen him a hundred times in my dreams."

Peter held out his hand. "Hello, Father O'Neil. My name is Peter Cash. I must apologize and ask your forgiveness; it is my fault you are here."

Tom frowned. "I'm sorry. I don't understand what you mean."

"You will, Tom," Mary Ann said. "We have only fifteen minutes to talk. Let's all have a seat."

"All right, Father," Peter said after they had taken a seat at the far end of the table, away from the guard. "I've told your family the truth. I know you didn't get Miss Josephine McCourt pregnant. I did. She paid me to do it, and after it was done, she put the blame on you. Your mother has told me that for some time now she has been trying to raise money to retry your case. I'll help you, first by paying for the retrial, and also by testifying against that woman. I only hope that you can forgive me for what I have done to you."

Tom smiled and laid a hand on Peter's arm. "I do. For seven years now you've been trying to tell me something. I could never figured out what it was. Tell me, Peter. Was there a baby?"

"I didn't see one with her on the train."

"We've already started, Tom," Mary Ann said. "We talked to a lawyer, and he is working on getting you out of here as we speak."

"All right, Mother, but don't get your hopes up too high. You're dealing with powerful people who've never lost."

"Well, their luck is about to change. The lawyer told us that he's suspected what has been going on in the McCourt business for years. The justice department has been cleaned up, and most of the crooked officials who were in power seven years ago are not there anymore.

"He said he wasn't a hundred per cent sure he could clear you of the charges, but he said there is a good chance."

The guard was coming their way. Tom stood and shook Peter's hand. "I want to thank you for your honesty, my friend. Be careful, and stay out of Fred and Josephine McCourt's way."

Peter smiled. "Don't worry. I will."

***

Trouble was brewing for Fred McCourt. He didn't know it, but Liam McCarthy, the lawyer Mary Ann O'Neil and Peter Cash hired, had been making inquiries to former justice department employees and he had made some startling discoveries. Apparently, substantial amounts of money had changed hands during their time in office, and now that they no longer held positions of power, neither of the two men who McCarthy had contacted felt they owed Fred McCourt anything.

Soon, Fred was feeling boxed in and knew he had to do something. Mr. Rourke, his own lawyer, had contacted him and warned him that some old friends had lately begun to feel unappreciated. Various associates were now under investigation for suspicion of accepting bribes, while others whom they had blackmailed were coming under pressure from the authorities to reveal their creditors. They hadn't answered any of his correspondence, so Rourke notified McCourt that a trip to the city very soon might be in order. There was nothing to worry about, Mr. Rourke told him, just as long as he headed off any further complications. He would bring more money as his lawyer advised, and as a contingency plan, he decided he would bring his pistol.

Jo was amused at her father's agitation over the following two weeks. She didn't know exactly what was bothering him and in truth didn't want to know. Most likely it had something to do with someone her father had either paid off or threatened to further his many lucrative business enterprises. He was careless, that was his problem. Jo felt no pity for anyone who couldn't cover his own tracks, even if he was her father.

She had only a passing knowledge of some of the crooked deals her father was involved in. The Minister of Justice had taken his own life; that much was public knowledge, as was the ongoing investigation of some of his colleagues. Jo wondered if her father was one of those being investigated, but quickly dismissed the thought. His affairs were his own and had nothing to do with her.

If Fred were to wind up rotting away in some prison, everything would be hers: his money, his land, his businesses. She laughed when a certain irony occurred to her. What if her father landed himself in jail alongside one Father Tom O'Neil?

The day after Fred left to meet with his lawyer in the city, there came a knock on Jo's bedroom door.

"Miss Josephine," said the old serving lady, "two men are here to see you."

"Oh, what now? Jo said, irritated. "Tell them Father isn't here. I'm not running his errands."

"They asked to talk to you, miss."

Jo sighed and followed the maid downstairs. To her surprise, the two men were lawmen. One of them held an envelope.

"Are you Josephine McCourt?"

"I am. What can I do for you?"

The man with the envelope handed it to her and said, "Miss Josephine McCourt, you are to appear at the church in O'Neil's Landing two weeks from this day, Wednesday morning, 10:00 A.M., to serve as a witness in the appeal of Father Thomas O'Neil's case."

"What? Is this some kind of joke?"

"No ma'am," the lawman said. "It has been decided by the judge that two weeks will be sufficient time for you to get yourself a lawyer and prepare for the case."

This was all coming at her a little too fast. "I don't understand. What are you talking about?"

"Tom O'Neil has been granted a new trial, and court will be held at the church."

Jo's eyes widened. "How is this possible? Don't you have to have new evidence to get a second trial?"

The smirk on the lawman's face betrayed his opinions of Jo and her father. "Well he's got some now, and from what I hear it is very strong."

Jo blinked.

"Yes," the man continued blandly, "that O'Neil lad isn't at the prison anymore, either. He is over in the jail at O'Neil's Landing right now."

"Not for long," Jo said in an icy tone as the two lawmen went out the front door. She slammed it behind them.

I have to calm down, she thought. *I can't let them get to me.* Getting angry only made her look guilty. She had to think of something, and fast. How was it possible the priest had been granted a retrial?

She retraced the events leading up to Tom's conviction, everyone from the night she had propositioned him at his parish house. The housekeeper had left and couldn't have witnessed anything. The stranger she had hired to take her to the cabin was a distant memory. The midwife her father had paid to take care of her and the baby once it was born wouldn't have dared cross the McCourt family. What, or who, did Father Tom have up his sleeve?

There was very little time. She would need a lawyer, and lucky for her the best one in the country was on her father's payroll. Fred was in trouble and no doubt would need his lawyer's aid in the near future, but his legal problems would just have to have to wait in line. Jo needed help now, her father be damned.

Chapter 23

TWO DAYS BEFORE the court work, Liam McCarthy drove out to the O'Neil farm. Mary Ann met him at the door and invited him in. They sat down to a cup of tea just as her sons came inside. The lawyer greeted William and David. "Hello. I was just about to tell your mother that there's a very good chance your brother will soon be a free man."

William shook the man's hand. "This is wonderful news!"

McCarthy continued. "I was asking for a lot of money to take on this case. To tell you the truth, at first I didn't think we would stand a chance of winning it. But new things have come to light about your son and even about Fred and Jo McCourt. I'll work on the case for no more than the cost of my expenses. It would be reward enough to put those inhumane people behind bars."

Mary Ann couldn't speak. She just looked at him with tears in her eyes.

"I can't tell you what will be said in court on Wednesday, but I want you three to be prepared for any surprises. That lawyer of theirs is a sneaky one." He laughed. "Just once I'd like to see him lose a case. And I think this time he will."

He stood, picked up his hat and went to the door. Mary Ann got up from the table and gave him a warm hug. "Thank you. Without you and Peter Cash, my son would spend the next eight years in that prison. He's dying in there, you know. It's a horrible place, and I wouldn't wish it on anyone, even the McCourts."

"Only time will tell, Mrs. O'Neil," McCarthy said.

Mary Ann awoke Wednesday morning to sunlight pouring into her room. She couldn't remember ever having slept so well. For years her dreams were haunted by the vision of a son she couldn't save. Her boys would be standing with her in the courtroom, but she also felt the strength of generations past flowing through her as well.

It saddened her that her husband hadn't lived to see their son become a priest, but somehow she was sure that he knew. Tom had so much of his father in him, and his grandfather as well.

Grandfather. She remembered her husband's words as they had stood in the cemetery. Grandfather's presence continued to sustain her, even from beyond the grave. In her childhood, she had been tormented by a man's face she couldn't remember, but one she couldn't forget.

Her own parents she never knew, only that they had died when she was but an infant. A mysterious man had come to her rescue; her parents were dead beside her, and it was only a matter of time before she joined them. She lived her whole life not knowing the man who rescued her from the cabin and placed her in the loving arms of the Kennedys. Grandfather had said that God Himself had a hand in her rescue.

Kitchen smells brought Mary Ann out of her reverie. Fresh biscuits, fried eggs, steaming ham, and tea were waiting for her in the kitchen. She dressed and went downstairs to join her daughters-in-law.

All at the table gave thanks to God for their meal before eating.

"There's only one thing missing," David said.

"I know," Mary Ann said. "He'll be here tomorrow morning."

After they ate, the three went outside and readied a team of horses to take them to town. They arrived and had to push their way through a huge crowd, larger than the one that had accompanied Father Tom's first trial in the church. They went inside, and Mary Ann took a seat while David and William mingled with the crowd. When they returned and took their seats next to their mother, David leaned toward his mother and whispered, "Some people even brought their own chairs. They are expecting something big to happen today."

"David," she said, "the only thing I want to see happen here today is my son made a free man."

At nine-fifteen, two fine black stallions pulling an elaborate carriage pulled up in front of the courthouse. Written across the rig in a delicate script was written the word JO. The carriage door opened, and the crowd that had accumulated in front of the courthouse began to talk excitedly. The beautiful Josephine McCourt stepped down from her carriage and strutted through the crowd, not deigning to meet anyone's eye, her chin thrust out proudly.

There were no outward emotions as she made her way up the aisle, but inside, Jo was a bundle of nerves. All the necessary preparations had been made. Mr. Rourke had assured her that nothing the O'Neils could produce would change the fact that she had been alone with the priest that night, and that she *had* become pregnant. This was physical evidence that could not be refuted. Yet Jo was outraged that the priest's family had dared to force her to suffer through this indignity again. She decided at that moment, as hundreds of people continued staring and pointing at her, that she would leave this place for good. This trial would be over in minutes, and she would say goodbye to these peasants forever. She had packed her belongings and put them in her carriage, fully planning to depart town immediately following the trial.

Still, she hadn't seen or heard from her father since he had gone to the city, and this worried her. She had rifled through his various ledgers and accounts to find the names of some of his contacts and had sent word to each of them to inquire of his whereabouts. None could tell her where he was.

Maybe he was dead. Jo knew that her father was not above blackmailing those who stood in his way, and it was not inconceivable that one of these unfortunates had taken the law in his own hands and done away with him. When the possibility that her father had met an early demise crossed her mind, Jo didn't feel any sorrow at all. She felt relieved, actually.

Mr. Rourke came out of a side room and beckoned. In her present mood, Jo nearly raised her voice, but held her tongue. This man was here to help her, she reminded herself. But she still retained her icy veneer. He had disagreed when Jo suggested she take the stand first. She wanted to get this over with as soon as possible, but Rourke had warned her that the judge might not go along with it. Her story should be saved for last anyway, to reinforce the impact the rape had had on her.

She stepped into the small room and Rourke closed the door behind them. Then she turned, and the look she levelled at him made him pale visibly.

"What is it?" she snarled.

Mr. Rourke cleared his throat. "Miss Josephine, I must insist one last time that you not take the stand first. We don't want Tom's bleeding-heart story to be the last thing the judge hears before he makes his decision."

"Look," Jo snapped. "I've had just about enough of you. What am I paying you for, anyway?"

Mr. Rourke sighed. "Did the priest have a witness?"

"How do I know? I don't think so. Father and I took care of everything. Why don't you go ask him, if you can find him? Now get in there and stop bothering me." With that, she pushed past him and went into the courtroom.

Mr. Rourke watched her leave. Fred McCourt would never have talked to him like that. He shook his head. This was one case he felt he wouldn't mind losing.

Chapter 24

TOM COULDN'T RECALL the last time he had slept so well. The past few nights in O'Neil's Landing's jail seemed luxurious compared to his many restless nights at St. William's. No moans of sickness or pain or fear or loud screams of madness from other cells interrupted his sleep on the eve of his retrial. Though freedom seemed close at hand, before turning in toward the wall to let sleep overtake him, he prayed and asked God to watch over the poor neglected souls who called St. William's Jail home.

Cold seeped into the bones at St. William's. Swinging pickaxes every day made the inmates' muscles ache, the gruel they were fed left them lingering just this side of starvation, guards' laughter and barked orders broke a man's spirit, but the worst of all was the cold. A thin blanket was all a prisoner was given to ward off the chill, and Tom had spent many nights huddled in a corner with it wrapped around him, shivering and wondering if he would see morning again.

They were like sacks of potatoes stuffed in a cellar and forgotten. It was a miserable existence, one from which many would not escape. Tom would often think of his old roommate at the monastery, Robert Green. The poor young man had neither the will nor the discipline needed to survive the test and had elected to end his own life. Tom pitied him and prayed for him often following his death, but it was not until he was incarcerated himself and put in this place that he truly understood how a man could feel defeated. Every passing day brought Robert no peace, and temptation crept into his soul, to end the torment once and for all. But that was not Tom's way. He had spent the last seven years living as his grandfather would have wanted, trusting in God.

The morning of his second trial, a guard came to his cell and let himself in. "I have orders to take you to the hotel to clean up and have breakfast."

Surprised, Tom nodded. He held out his hands.

The guard shook his head. "There won't be any need for cuffs this morning, will there?" he said.

"I won't try to escape, if that's what you mean."

The guard blushed and looked at the ground. "Father, I'm sorry for what happened to you. I'm not the only one who thinks that you're innocent. If I had a say in the matter, you would be a free man today. And maybe you will be."

Tom and the guard exited the jail and went up the street to the hotel. They entered one of the rooms and were greeted by another guard."

After breakfast, which was brought to his room, Father Tom felt better than he had in a long time. The guard handed him a travel bag. "There are some clothes in here for you. You can change in the bathroom."

Tom entered the bathroom, and opened the bag to pull out a black suit. For a moment he didn't recognize the clothing, and then it dawned on him. This was the same suit Bishop Brown had given him upon graduation from the monastery. He reached in the bag and pulled out the white collar.

The guard had offered him the chance to enter the courtroom with dignity.

He dressed, and when he went outside the guard was holding the black hat Tom had also once worn, and this he handed to the priest.

The church was just as he remembered it. A flood of memories came back to him as he walked down the centre aisle and took a seat near the altar. It seemed like only yesterday that he was judged in this very place, and now, seven years later, he would be judged again.

Tom was heartened at the sight of many familiar faces in the crowd, and even more so by the smiles that brightened them. If they were one time uncertain as to whether he was guilty of the crime of which he was accused, most of them appeared to be on his side now. He sought out the faces of his mother and brothers, and when he found them he folded his hands and held them up. He smiled when they returned the gesture; he knew they were praying for him.

At ten o'clock, all rose as the judge entered to begin the jury selection. Tom looked in the direction of Josephine McCourt and Rourke several times, but neither acknowledged him and kept looking straight ahead.

The judge banged his gavel on his makeshift desk and looked at Jo's lawyer. "I understand your client wishes to take the stand first."

"Yes, Your Honour," Mr. Rourke replied.

"Are there any objections?" the judge asked McCarthy.

"No, Your Honour."

"Very well. Miss McCourt, you may proceed."

Jo took the stand and gave her oath to tell the truth. Then Rourke stood and asked her in a confident voice, "Miss McCourt, would you please tell this court what happened the night you went to see Father Tom O'Neil at his parish house?"

Jo nodded. The look she wore was one of abject despair. She hung her head and recounted, word for word, the same story she had given the court seven years before. Rourke thanked her when she finished, and he sat down.

"Do you have any questions for this witness?" the judge asked McCarthy.

"I do, Your Honour." He winked at Tom, then stood and walked to the witness stand. He cleared his throat.

"Miss McCourt, is it true that you left for the city early the morning after you visited Father Tom O'Neil at his house?"

"I ... I don't remember," Jo said.

"You don't remember? Yet you remember every little detail of the parish house?"

Jo nodded quickly. "Yes, now I remember. I did go to the city sometime after that."

"Didn't you leave very early the next morning? Think, now."

"Yes."

"And during your travels, did you happen upon a young man at a campground commonly known as Halfway?"

Jo paled. She glanced toward Rourke, then answered. "No."

"And, Miss McCourt," McCarthy said, turning to give the crowd a meaningful look, "Isn't it true that you paid this young man a sum of one thousand pounds to spend two nights with you? With the intention of getting yourself pregnant?"

"What?" Jo screamed. "No!"

"And isn't it true you promised him another one thousand pounds if he did not mention ever having met you?"

"No," she said, calmly this time. "No, it isn't true."

"Was there a baby?" McCarthy asked in a low voice.

Jo looked at Rourke. His face was impassive, unreadable.

The judge spoke up. "Answer the question, Miss McCourt."

Jo's eyes snapped back and met McCarthy's gaze again. "Yes. It belongs to Tom O'Neil."

"And where is this child?"

"I ... don't know."

"May I remind you, Miss McCourt, that you are under oath? I will ask you one more time. Did you pay a young man one thousand pounds to have sexual relations with you?"

"No," she said, gritting her teeth. "There was no young man, and there was no money."

"Very well. I have no more questions for this witness. Your Honour, I would like to call Peter Cash to the stand."

Toward the back of the church, Peter stood and made his way to the front. He gave Jo a frosty look as he passed, and when she saw him her mouth fell open. She recognized him this time.

When he took the stand, McCarthy said, "Mr. Cash, in your own words would you please tell this court what happened the day you first met Miss Josephine McCourt?"

"Certainly," Peter said. "I've been trying to live with this guilt for seven years. I'm not proud of what I did, and now I see that someone else was made to pay for it.

"On the day in question, I was making tea and resting at the campground you mentioned. A carriage pulled up as I was stirring the kettle, and the woman sitting in the carriage got down and came over to the fire. She asked me if I wanted company, and I said

I wouldn't mind. Well, she told me soon after that she was looking for someone to do a job for her.

"I asked what she needed done, and she told me she wanted to spend the next two nights with me in the cabin just a little ways up the road. I was shocked ... but I accepted her offer. I thought there was something odd about it, though, when she offered to pay me. Not only that, she said there was more money where that came from if I promised to keep my mouth shut about the whole thing."

The courtroom had fallen deathly silent at this point. Everyone seemed to be holding his breath. Then McCarthy asked, "And why are you only coming forward now?"

Peter sighed. "As I said, I've felt guilty over what I did with that woman for a long time. I felt so bad, I couldn't even bring myself to spend the money she gave me.

"I sell farm machinery, and not long ago I got on the train to Armagh to build a new client list for my employer. After I left Miss McCourt years ago, I never thought I'd see her again. But there she was, on the same train."

McCarthy interrupted. "You're absolutely sure the woman you met seven years ago is in this courtroom today?"

Peter looked at Jo. "Yes, that's her. I never forgot her face—especially those eyes."

"So I asked around and found out that she was from O'Neil's Landing. That's when I remembered the story that was in all the newspapers years ago, about a priest who was up on charges of rape. It didn't take long to find out that Miss McCourt was the woman who accused Father Tom O'Neil of that crime.

"It all made sense to me then: why she wanted to get pregnant, and why she needed me to stay quiet about it. I don't know why she wanted to hurt Father O'Neil so badly—

"Objection, Your Honour," Mr. Rourke said suddenly. Until now he had been silent. Jo sat stock-still beside him, frightened and furious at the same time. "This is a lovely story, lovely indeed. But what this Mr. Cash is suggesting is preposterous. Everyone in this court can plainly see that my client is an attractive young woman. I defy any man here to say he would turn down an offer from her such as Mr. Cash has stated. To suggest that she paid to have a man bed her is absurd.

"My client has never so much as laid eyes on this man before today. This is obviously a desperate attempt by the O'Neil family to discredit Miss McCourt. She was assaulted by the defendant seven years ago, she became pregnant by him as was testified by my expert witness, and she has lived all these years in shame for something that was not her fault.

"Hasn't my client suffered enough? The only truth that has been revealed today is just how vicious the O'Neils can be. In fact, it is my opinion that, in some last-ditch effort to free a man who anyone with a shred of intelligence or human decency can clearly see is guilty, it was not my client who paid this witness to keep silent, but it was the O'Neils who paid him to *tell* this story."

Mr. Rourke was red in the face, and frothing at the mouth. "If there is nothing more, Your Honour, I *demand* that my client not be further subjected to this sideshow the O'Neils have fabricated." He sat down and glared at McCarthy.

The judge squared his shoulders and looked at Peter Cash. "You may step down." Turning to face McCarthy, he said, "I'm inclined to agree with Mr. Rourke. Your client has admitted to seeing Miss McCourt the night she went to the parish house, and later she discovered she was pregnant. You need solid evidence to back up Peter Cash's story."

Several people in the crowd shouted in outrage, and soon all the gathered people filled the church with a steady rumble of protest and indignation. The judge smacked his gavel upon his desk several times in quick succession, and the din gradually subsided to a murmur, then stopped.

"Do you have anything else?" the judge asked McCarthy.

"Actually, Your Honour, I do. I would like to call my last witness to the stand now."

People turned toward the back of the church to see this new witness. The doors opened, and the crowd was in shock. Fred McCourt was being led up the aisle by two policemen. He was shackled at the wrists and ankles.

Chapter 25

IF ANYONE IN O'NEIL'S Landing were asked the reason for the McCourt family's ill will toward the O'Neils, he wouldn't be able to tell you. He would shrug and dismiss it as the general contempt of moneyed people for the working class. The McCourts were opportunists who would stoop to any level, he would say, using any means to remove those who stood in their way. Their bloodline was tainted with greed and corruption. None were exempt from their ruthlessness, and anyone you asked would say that the O'Neils had simply found themselves in the wrong place at the wrong time.

Fred was hated by many, not only in this town but elsewhere in Ireland as well. But he had been lucky throughout his career, and most who wished to see him imprisoned for shady business activities were corrupt themselves. Their silence could be bought or extorted. The innocents who found themselves on the receiving end of Fred's wrath could only watch in helpless frustration as liens were put on their properties, or frivolous lawsuits ended up on their doorsteps that threatened to tie them up in litigation for years. Close relatives suddenly found themselves jobless and unable to get work, or in the case of merchants and farmers, markets mysteriously dried up.

James McCourt had been a tactical genius when it came to getting what he wanted. Growing up, his son Fred had developed a great respect for the old man, whom he believed was the most powerful man in all of Ireland. People did what he told them to do; professionals from all walks of life—merchants, physicians, teachers, lawyers, even judges—feared the man. In his declining years, James passed to Fred, his most eager pupil, many of the secrets of his success.

Yes, James had been a criminal mastermind in his day. But it was not always so.

Fred sat in a small, dimly lit room in a basement. For the first time in his life, he was scared. Several lawmen had escorted him here and left him alone with his thoughts for over an hour.

The door opened, and two burly men walked in. One pulled up a chair, while the other stood motionless to Fred's left.

"Now, Fred," the man sitting across from him said, "you can help yourself by helping us. From what we hear, you've been a very busy man for the past thirty years.

"The whole justice department is being investigated even as I say this. You and everyone else in this city has heard by now that the Minister committeed suicide. What I want to know is why. You can start at the beginning if you wish, or anywhere at all. I'm a patient man."

He must think I'm stupid, Fred thought. *If they had anything on me, I'd be charged.*

Rourke, his lawyer, wasn't present, but Fred knew enough about the law to know he didn't have to say anything. Still, it irritated him to learn that his daughter had taken his lawyer away when he needed someone in his corner. He swore under his breath and promised to punish her when he got back to his estate.

"Fred."

He looked at the lawman.

"I'm afraid Bill here isn't as patient as I am." Turning to the burly guard, he said, "Let him have it."

My God, thought Fred. *Are they going to beat it out of me?*

When James McCourt was in his prime, he fell in love with a young woman from O'Neil's Landing. Peggy Stewart was a beautiful lady, born into a merchant family and full of promise. James had come from a modest family, and though he knew marrying into Peggy's family would provide a comfortable living for him, he thought only of her and the family they would one day raise themselves.

James worked hard day and night for his future father-in-law, travelling across the country and meeting with the old man's clients and making new contacts along the way. He was good at what he did. Peggy's father saw great potential in him, and sometimes when they celebrated over a belt of single malt, the old man would express his gratitude and tell James what a fine addition he would make to the family.

Fred and Peggy were madly in love. They attended all the times in O'Neil's Landing and mingled with other well-to-do couples. The two young lovers were the talk of the town. It was said a handsomer couple couldn't be found in all of County Armagh.

Young James McCourt was a dynamo, a charmer. The business flourished while he was under Mr. Stewart's wing, and it was not long before the old guy confided that he would leave the business to him. James was elated. He had everything he had ever wanted in life: a fine woman, a promising career, and a future for his family.

"If you cooperate, we will forget the rape charge," said Bill, the lawman standing over him.

"What rape charge?" Fred stammered.

"Fred, don't play games. We know all about the girl you raped back in ... when was it? I believe you were sixteen years old at the time. Your father owned the judge. You know it, and we know it."

Fred actually laughed at him. "What? You can't prove anything, *sir*. That case was thrown out. Now, if you gentlemen want anything else from me, you'll have to go through my lawyer."

Bill motioned to the other lawman, and they left the room. When they were alone, Bill started to chuckle. "Did you see the look on his face, Paddy? I thought he was going to wet himself."

"Yes. He may think he's got us, but it's about to get a lot worse for him."

"You mean ... ?"

Paddy nodded. "He's sunk. I was talking to the O'Neil lawyer; he's made our jobs a whole lot easier. We have him on several counts of extortion and bribery now, and a lot more."

"Why don't we just arrest him?"

"Not yet, Bill. We want Fred to help us with something else first."

Two years after James McCourt began working for Mr. Stewart, the old man took sick. He drew James aside one day and said, "I'm not going to be around much longer, but I know my Peggy will be taken care of. I want you to take over the business now, my boy. I know you'll do me proud."

And so the old man signed all the necessary paperwork with a witness present, and James McCourt became the sole proprietor of the business. He and Peggy spent the next few months near the old man. Mr. Stewart was failing fast, and when his time came, he left this world with an easy mind.

James did his best to console his girlfriend, but she had fallen into a depressed state and couldn't be reasoned with. Never one to give up, he worked hard at his business and put off travelling for a while so he could take care of Peggy and her mother. However, as time passed, James began to feel more and more that his lady's heart was not set on marrying him anymore.

James started travelling again, partly to re-establish old contacts and obtain more clients for himself, but also to give Peggy some time alone. He couldn't help her by hovering over her all the time, he decided. Each time he travelled, he stayed away for longer periods than the last. He missed Peggy, but he didn't know what else to do.

The two lawmen, Paddy and Bill, went back in the interrogation room to see Fred smiling triumphantly with his arms folded. Paddy gave Bill a smirk, then took his seat again across from Fred.

"You're right, Fred," said Paddy. "You don't have to say anything if you don't want to. But I think that you *will* want to after you hear what I have to say."

"Oh, really?"

"Really. If you cooperate, you just may save yourself from hanging."

Fred grunted. "How do I know I can trust you?"

"You don't," Bill interrupted. "But you're going to have to, just like we have to trust you."

Paddy nodded. "Your father James was a real heavy hitter back in the old days, wasn't he?"

"Yes."

"But he was also a murderer."

Fred's eyes widened. "What?" he shouted.

"We know," Paddy said, his eyes boring into Fred's like hot pokers. "You know it, too, which makes you an accessory after the fact."

Fred shifted in his seat. "I don't know—"

"Save yourself the trouble," Paddy snapped. "Your only choice now is whether you want to hang or go to jail."

Fred's forehead broke out in a sweat. "What ... what do you want from me?"

Paddy looked up at Bill, then back at Fred. "We want you to tell us what happened between your daughter and Father Tom O'Neil seven years ago."

James spent more and more time away from Peggy over the next two years. Each time he returned from his business trips, he would find her holed up in her family's house with her mother. She had grown despondent, and forewent all the social gatherings that had so marked her and James's relationship.

Peggy and her mother lived as recluses, and James was at a loss. He felt an obligation to provide for them as he always had, and he kept on with the business. For all his failure to win back Peggy's affection, the undertaking that had once been a modest-sized merchandising firm under the care of Mr. Stewart now knew success the old man had never dreamed of when he was alive. James McCourt was becoming a household name in the commercial field, and even ambitious, politically motivated individuals were starting to take notice of the brilliant entrepreneur.

James received invitations to dine with dignitaries all over the country. He was reluctant to accept; he knew that, should his future take a political turn, he would have less time to spend out in the field, tapping new markets and marking new territory along the way. His buyers trusted and respected him; he never took advantage and always sought fair prices with little profit margin for himself. In time, Peggy would see what an important man he had become.

One day, after a particularly long time away from home, James returned to find Peggy in better spirits. No longer content to spend her days in the home, she had taken to attending social events again and renewing old friendships. James was overjoyed. Finally, after years of waiting for his Peggy to come back to him, they could wed and enjoy the prosperity he had won.

But Peggy had other plans. Her days and nights socializing had initially been her mother's idea. Widow Stewart did not like seeing her daughter wasting her youth at home watching the world pass her by. She had urged her daughter to go out and enjoy life before it was too late. Life went on, she had said, and her father would not have wanted to see her wasting her time. She owed it to herself, and to James.

When Peggy attended her first party after her years-long hiatus, she had felt out of place. The others looked so happy, and this mildly affronted her. But as time went on, she became more at ease in the company of other revellers, and soon she spent nearly every night out on the town.

Matt Jones was everything Peggy was not. He was a farmer, handsome to be sure, but poor nonetheless. They met at a dance one night when the well-to-do party-goers had been feeling particularly rowdy and in need of a little adventure. Despite his meagre earnings, Matt's simple charm and easy smile won Peggy over, and soon the two were courting. James had come home to find the woman he was to marry in company with another man.

    James McCourt became a very bitter man. He moved out of the house he shared with the Stewarts and rented a place in O'Neil's Landing. Soon, there were plans underway to construct an estate on the outskirts of town to serve as his permanent residence. Old man Stewart had signed everything over to him—his land, his house, his business—and, feeling he owed Peggy no more, his first act upon moving into his estate was to put the house she was living in up for sale.

    In a short time, the house was sold, and Peggy and her mother were left to fend for themselves. Years later, James heard that his once future mother-in-law had died a lonely old woman in the poorhouse.

    Peggy and Matt were wed, and having no prospects in this town, moved away and in time were forgotten by all but James.

"What happened to them?" asked Paddy the lawman.

    Fred looked nervously from Paddy to Bill, then said in a low voice, "They were poisoned."

    Bill nodded. "That sounds about right. The man and woman who were found in that cabin long ago were believed to have died from disease, but everyone was suspicious. The baby was healthy, and the father looked like he was trying to crawl to the door. If disease was what took him, most likely he would have been too weak to do even that."

    "Father tracked them down," said Fred. "He could have gotten anyone to do it, but he wanted to do away with them himself. So he poisoned their water."

"And what about the baby?" asked Paddy.

"That was the only problem," Fred replied. "He didn't realize there was a baby until it was too late, and he felt guilty about leaving her there.

"Father didn't want the baby to die, so he sent Rourke out that same day to bring her to safety."

"Thank you for clearing up that great mystery, Fred," said Paddy. "There's one more thing. Did Father O'Neil rape your daughter seven years ago?"

"No."

"Are you willing to take the stand and testify to that effect?"

"Yes."

"Good," said Paddy. "Your father saved Mary Ann O'Neil's life many years ago, and now it looks like you're going to do the same for her son."

Chapter 26

He looked like a very old man as he sat and told the people in the courtroom of things they knew nothing about.

Fred McCourt admitted to blackmailing justice officials, bribery, and to his daughter's framing of Father Tom O'Neil. He also confessed that his father fabricated the rape charge years ago for the purpose of driving the young woman's family from their land.

When Fred was led back to his seat from the witness box, the judge spoke. "The jury has heard everything, and I now ask them to retire and come back with a verdict. Court is dismissed for lunch." Fred was sent to the lockup, and Jo was supervised by one of the guards.

When court resumed, the judge asked the jury if it had reached a verdict.

"We have, your honour."

"Will the defendant please rise?"

The foreman of the jury spoke. "We find the defendant not guilty."

The courtroom erupted in cheers as neighbours slapped each other on the back, celebrating the comeuppance of McCourt and freedom for Father O'Neil. The judge banged his gavel to restore order.

He looked at Tom. "Do you intend to press charges against Miss Josephine?"

"No, Your Honour. She is more to be pitied than chastised."

"Well, the court has to press charges of perjury. Father O'Neil, you're free to go."

Tom turned to his mother and said, "God's law has saved me ... saved us all."

Across the room, lawmen were shackling Josephine McCourt. Tom knew the feeling of iron bands around his wrists.

Tom returned home for the first time in seven years, and revelled in setting foot on the farm once again.

He returned to celebrating Mass at the church in O'Neil's Landing and his mother returned once again to the parish house to help Tom, while his brothers and their families continued to live on the farm.

He made a promise that he would help those men in the prison as much as possible by personal visits, and forever included them in his prayers.

Peter Cash returned to his job as a travelling salesman, but would visit the O'Neils at least a couple of times a year.

Fred and Jo were sent to prison, ending the McCourt dynasty.

From that time forward, whenever he spoke of the gifts of God in his sermons, Father Tom meant the land, his family, and friends such as Johnny Connors.

Gordon Walsh is the second oldest in a family of eleven children born to John and Bertha Lewis Walsh of Fleur de Lys. He fished with his father out of Fleur de Lys before working in the lumber camps for Bowaters of Corner Brook. He also fished on the Labrador for two years.

He is married to the former Clotilda Quigley, and they have four daughters and one son. After ten years as a heavy equipment operator in the Baie Verte asbestos mine, the author returned to fishing for ten years. He was later employed with the town council of Fleur de Lys.

His first book, *Into the Night: The Samantha Walsh Story*, released in 2002, quickly became a Canadian Best-Seller.